Simply KAT McCRUMBLE

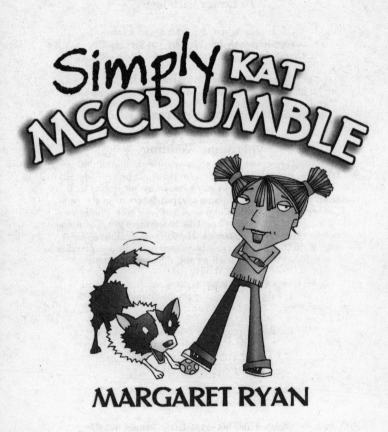

MARGARET RYAN

Hodder
Children's
Books

A division of Hodder Headline Limited

To Lesley with love

Text copyright © 2005 Margaret Ryan
Illustrations copyright © 2005 Jan McCafferty
First published in 2005 by Hodder Children's Books

The rights of Margaret Ryan and Jan McCafferty
to be identified as the Author and Illustrator of the work
respectively have been asserted by them in accordance
with the Copyright, Designs and Patents Act 1988.

2 4 6 8 10 9 7 5 3 1

A Catalogue record for this book is available
from the British Library

ISBN 0 340 88401 0

Typeset in Baskerville by Avon DataSet Ltd,
Bidford-on-Avon, Warwickshire

Printed and bound in Great Britain by
Bookmarque Ltd, Croydon, Surrey

The paper and board used in this paperback are natural
recyclable products made from wood grown in sustainable
forests. The manufacturing processes conform to the
environmental regulations of the country of origin.

Hodder Children's Books
A division of Hodder Headline Limited
338 Euston Road
London NW1 3BH

Scottish for Beginners

Auchtertuie: the village where I live. I know it looks a little like a giant sneeze, but you can say it. Honest. Try . . . OCH-TER-2-Y. See. Easy.

Bannocks: round flat cakes made with oatmeal and flour. Yummy.

Cranachan: pronounced 'CRA-NA-KAN'. Tipsy pudding made with raspberries, toasted oatmeal, double cream, honey and whisky. Hic. Sorry. Pardon!

Gang aft agley: often go wrong. Like your schemes to get more pocket money from your mum.

MSP: Member of the Scottish Parliament. They hang out in Edinburgh and only occasionally wear kilts.

Plaid: pronounced 'PLAD'. Rectangular length of woollen cloth usually in tartan. Now only worn as ceremonial dress by people in pipe bands, and daft folk at weddings.

Tapsalteerie: state of confusion. Like your bedroom maybe? (Certainly like mine! *author*.)

A wee tate: a small amount of something. Like a wee tate of sugar in your tea or honey in your porridge.

Chapter 1

Hi, I'm Kat. Not Katy or Kate, but Kat. Kat McCrumble. My full name is Katriona Mhairi McConnell McCrumble, after my paternal great-grandmother; so you can see why I just like to be called Kat. But I suppose it could be worse. I heard the other day about a girl called Annette Curtin, and a boy called Dwain Pipe. Why do parents give their children names like that? Do they think it's funny? Have they no idea what it's like to go through school with everyone laughing? Honestly, it makes me mad that some parents can be so stupid. The Nisbet boys, who live on a nearby hill farm, once called me Ginger Nut. But only once. I threatened to send the ghost of the Crumbling

Arms to haunt them, and they stopped. Sharpish.

That's where I live: the Crumbling Arms inn, Auchtertuie, Scotland. Our ghost Old Hamish lives there too. He and I are good friends and, once you get used to him, he's not really that scary. But the Nisbet boys don't know that.

Old Hamish is one of my McCrumble ancestors. He comes complete with old McCrumble tartan kilt and plaid, but I'll tell you more about him later.

I also live with my dad, Hector. He comes incomplete. Mislays his memory sometimes. But, with my help, and especially my memory, he runs the Crumbling Arms inn, as well as a sanctuary for wild animals, as well as holiday homes for pets. Just in case all this sounds a bit posh, I can tell you it's not. The Crumbling Arms is slowly crumbling, and the wildlife sanctuary and holiday homes in our back yard are made up of runs and pens we've made ourselves. They don't look fantastic, but the animals are happy. Dad and I plan to have a proper wildlife sanctuary one day, with custom-built accommodation. We're saving up as best we can, but the Crumbling Arms doesn't make much money, so it may take a while.

We do have some help, of course, since I, unfortunately, have to go to school – a necessary evil if I want to be a vet – which I do. The folks who help us are McCrumbles too, and all related in some way.

There's a little bit of north-west Scotland, not far from Fort William, just north of the Great Glen, that's McCrumble country. That makes it sound a bit like the Wild West, doesn't it, but it's more rain and midges than cacti and coyotes. Anyway, a pile of McCrumbles live there. I don't know what the collective noun is for a pile of McCrumbles; possibly just a pile of McCrumbles. Or, it might be a *grumble* of McCrumbles, especially when the wind finds the chinks in our anoraks and the sleet turns our cheeks to scarlet. Never a *humble* of McCrumbles because we can be a proud, fiery lot – goes with the red hair. And never a *mumble* of McCrumbles for we've usually got plenty to say for ourselves. Possibly a *rumble* of McCrumbles, though the rumble can easily turn to a roar when we're annoyed.

One of the quieter McCrumbles though is Donald, our handyman. He's a part-time fixer of anything broken and a part-time druid. Some people find him strange. The white frock can confuse them, but he's the gentlest, kindest man around, along with my dad. Donald cares passionately about animals and trees. He spends a lot of his time up in trees. He hugs them, talks to them and generally looks after them, especially the ones on the big estate which stretches for miles behind the Crumbling Arms. Some of the trees on the estate are very old and Donald secretly takes care of them, making sure Ron Jackson, the horrible gamekeeper, never catches him. If Donald thinks a tree is poorly, he makes up a special medicinal mixture and spreads it round the roots. He's a kind of doc in a frock, I suppose.

Our cook, Kirsty, has a special recipe too when people are ailing or anxious. She blends kindness into her scone mix, and, even if her scones can't solve the problem, they certainly cheer it up. If Kirsty ruled the world, she'd sort out most of its problems with a cup of tea and some home baking. Sometimes, though, she has problems of her own, and, if they get too much, she resorts to her other remedy. Malt whisky. The bottle lives on our kitchen dresser inside the blue and white jar marked FLOUR. Fortunately Kirsty doesn't have to use this remedy on herself very often, for, when she does, she starts to sing. This frightens all the seagulls off Loch Bracken, and the sea trout dive for cover. Then, Lachy McCrumble, out on his boat, sadly packs up his fishing gear and goes home. Sometimes Kirsty even gets out her bagpipes and marches up and down the kitchen playing – well, we're never very sure what. But, no matter how much she practises, she'll still never get into the Auchtertuie pipe band.

It's the Auchtertuie Highland Games soon and the band will take the lead, heading up the competitors in the opening parade. There will be caber tossers, shotputters and highland dancers, as well as the tug-of-war teams and the wellie hurlers. They always take the same route along the lochside, past the Crumbling Arms. The pipe major stops for a wee dram before they head on through the village and up to the field where the Games are held. The field is at the foot of Ben Bracken, the mountain whose imposing presence looms over the Games. They can be very noisy and colourful on a fine day, with lots of music and dancing and people parading in their kilts.

The Games' organiser, Henry McCrumble, usually consults Morag, our postie, to find out if she knows what the weather is going to be like on Games day. Morag has the gift of the second sight and can sometimes 'see' things the rest of us can't. She can often tell you what's in your mail before you've even opened it. Like the other morning when she came into the kitchen of the Crumbling Arms for her usual cup of tea.

'Jinty McCrumble's niece in Inverness is going to have a baby,' she announced, pouring out her tea from the big brown pot that seems to live permanently on our table.

'Oh,' sniffed Kirsty, pausing in the middle of her soup making. 'That's strange. I was in the bakery this morning and Jinty never mentioned it.'

'She doesn't know about it yet,' smiled Morag, holding up a slim blue envelope. 'I haven't delivered the letter from her niece yet.'

'Ah,' said Kirsty, mollified, and carried on chopping her veggies.

No one is surprised by Morag's announcements now, and there are very few secrets in Auchtertuie.

If you were to pass through Auchtertuie on the bus or in a car, or even on foot if you were hiking, you might think, 'What a lovely place, nestling between the high Ben Bracken and the loch. How peaceful it looks. How quiet it is. I bet nothing much ever happens here.' You might think that, but you'd be wrong. Very wrong indeed. As you'll find out . . .

Chapter 2

The Crumbling Arms is never really quiet. Even if we have no guests, we always have the animals. They live in the pens and runs in the back yard and include Donk, our rescue donkey, and his girlfriend, Lily. They're really soppy about each other and spend a lot of time snuffling and nuzzling. They're worse than the soaps on TV. Actually, we're delighted for them. Donk was really badly treated by his last owner, and had to have an operation to remove his head collar which had become imbedded in his nose, but now he seems very happy. Lily thinks Donk is just wonderful and copies everything he does. He's her hero, even if he does have an odd-shaped conk.

Also in our pens at the moment is a rabbit called Lucy. Lucy's owner, Colin Dunlop, is away with his parents to Inverness to visit his granny in hospital. But he left me strict instructions about the care of his rabbit.

'Remember, Kat,' he said, trying to look as important as he could at age four years three days and twelve and a half minutes. 'Remember Lucy likes to sit in front of the fire and have her ears stroked. Remember that she doesn't like lettuce. Remember that she likes chocolate biscuits. Remember that Kit Kats are her favourite.'

I promised to remember. Lucy could share my Kit Kats. They were my favourite too.

We also have a young golden eagle to look after at the moment. That doesn't often happen. Donald found him at the edge of the forest at the back of the inn the other day, when he was out on his tree rounds. The eaglet was lying at the foot of a tree, completely stunned. Donald looked around and waited for a while, but there was no sign of the parents, so he picked the eaglet up gently and brought him to us.

Dad and I had a careful look at him, but we couldn't find anything broken. He just seemed a bit shocked. I don't know what had happened to him. Perhaps he wasn't looking where he was going and flew into a tree. Bit of a feather brain, maybe. Who knows? Anyway, we'll keep him for a few days till we're sure he's OK, then we'll release him. Probably take him closer to Ben Bracken where we know there are other golden eagles.

I've only ever seen one adult golden eagle up close. I was climbing the lower slopes of the Ben one day, puffing and panting behind Dad, when he stopped suddenly and motioned to me to be still. Then he pointed. Not far away a golden eagle sat perched on a dead tree-stump. He was a magnificent bird with piercing eyes and pale gold feathers at the back of his head. That's how golden eagles get their name. I watched him through Dad's binoculars till he stretched his huge wings with their finger-like ends and rose lazily into the air. Fantastic.

But our little eaglet has no golden feathers yet. He's still an all-over chocolate brown, so I called him Kit Kat. What else? It would be great to see him fly free. I just hope he looks where he's going from now on. Perhaps he'll have learned his lesson.

Mind you, Max never has. He's one of our Border collies. The other one, his mum, is called Millie. Millie is intelligent and one hundred per cent reliable. But Max? He must have been at the end of the queue when the brains were being handed out, and is about as reliable as a chocolate fireguard.

He and Millie live with us in the Crumbling Arms.

Everybody loves Millie, and customers have even asked if they could buy her from us. But Millie is not for sale. Not ever. Neither is Max, though no one has ever asked to buy him, funnily enough. Perhaps it's because he sneaks up to them in the bar and steals their crisps. Cheese and onion are his favourite, but too many of those and his breath is eye-watering. To say nothing of his other end. So I won't. He also suddenly remembers sometimes that he used to be a sheepdog. He gets a little look of concentration that means his one brain cell is sputtering into life and is telling him 'Herd, Max, herd'. So he does. In the absence of any sheep, he makes do with humans and herds them into the Crumbling Arms. It's one way to get customers, I suppose.

Another 'customer' who comes to visit us regularly is Flip. He's a badger who 'flips' his way through the cat flap on the back door of the inn and comes into the kitchen to eat Samantha's cat food.

Samantha's our other domestic pet, though she would hate to be called that. She is a very high-born Siamese cat, and lets us know it. She does 'haughty' really well – one of these days I'm going to take lessons from her – and only deigns to talk to us when she wants something. I read somewhere that in ancient Egypt, cats were considered goddesses. Well, Samantha must be descended from one, because she treats us mere mortals with disdain. A flick of her ears and wrinkle of her nose says it all.

I don't know whether she came from Egypt or not, more likely from a car that stopped, put her out and drove off. That's how we got her. Why do people do things like that? It makes me so mad when people treat animals like they were just so much rubbish to be disposed of.

I rant on about it to Dad sometimes. He always listens politely then says things like:

'Calm down, Kat. I agree with you.'

Or:

'Some people just need to be educated about animals, Kat.'

Or:

'If you feel so strongly, why don't you write a letter to your MSP?'

I tried that. He wrote back agreeing with me, but nothing else happened. Perhaps I'll be an MSP one day, as well as a vet. Then I'll get things changed, just see if I don't. Meantime, why people are rotten to animals is still a mystery to me.

Actually, come to think of it, there are a few

mysteries in my life, including: why do I have one foot bigger than the other, where do freckles come from, and why did they all land on me? Also, why are the best TV programmes on the night you have most homework? If you are a studious type of person, or a bit of a geek, or just your average, run-of-the-mill, minor genius, and know the answers to these mysteries, feel free to write. You can also include some mysteries/problems of your own, if you like. You know what they say, a problem shared is one that's all round the neighbourhood in no time.

So, Auchtertuie's my neighbourhood, then, and Dad and the people who help out at the Crumbling Arms are my family. The only person I haven't told you about yet is my best friend, Tina.

Chapter 3

My best friend's called Tina Morrison and she has a problem. Not odd-sized feet or freckles like me, but her family. They are all crazy, loopy, seriously bonkers type people. I think they're great, but Tina's not convinced. She sometimes says she wishes she'd been adopted, so she could claim she really wasn't related to her weird family at all. But if she thinks they're bad, she should try mine!

Tina and her family moved to Auchtertuie from London not long ago. They bought a run-down smallholding called Blain's farm, on the edge of the village. I met Tina and her family the very first day they moved in. Kirsty had sent me along with a basket of baking and some home-made strawberry jam to welcome them.

'I just noticed the big removal van at Blain's farm on my way past,' she'd said. 'That must be the new people moving in. Everything will be tapsalteerie along there so take this food and that will give them a bite to eat with their cup of tea.'

I took the basket. There were enough scones and fruit cake in there to feed a battalion.

I'd grinned and set off. I knew Kirsty was being her usual kind self. I also knew she wanted to know what the new people were like. I was nosey too. It's a McCrumble characteristic, along with the red hair and freckles.

The removal men were just carrying in an old spinning wheel when I got there, and a woman I assumed to be Mrs Morrison was directing them through to a back room.

'Set it down carefully,' she said. 'It mustn't be damaged.'

She smiled at me vaguely on the way past, as though I was possibly a child she'd forgotten she had, or maybe I'd come in with the furniture, or maybe I came with the house. I stood in the middle of the muddle and wondered what to do.

'Hi,' said a voice behind me. 'I'm Tina Morrison, who are you?'

'Kat McCrumble,' I said, and we both looked at each other and grinned. Funny how you just know you're going to like someone.

'I live at the Crumbling Arms,' I explained. 'Our cook, Kirsty, thought these might be useful.'

Tina looked doubtfully in the basket.

'Home-made scones and jam,' I explained. 'Kirsty's a wonderful cook.'

Tina's face cleared. 'Thank you very much,' she said. 'We can enjoy these. Mum's baking is disastrous. Tooth demolishing stuff. We went to a reconstructed Bronze Age village once and they had plaster replicas of the food people used to eat. Looked much better than what we get at home.'

'Too bad,' I sympathised. 'Tell me more about your family.'

We sat down on an old sofa the removal men brought in, and she did. At great length. Over half a basket of fruit scones and jam.

'We're not from round here,' she said. 'You might have guessed.'

'The accent's a bit of a giveaway,' I nodded.

'At least, Mum and I and Billy, that's my big brother, aren't Scottish, but my dad and his family are, from way back.'

I nodded again, using a finger to scoop up the jam that had dropped from a scone on to my sweatshirt. Good thing the sweatshirt was red anyway.

'And Dad's always wanted to get out of the big city to lead a different way of life. He's fed up with long hours at the office and long hours on the train. Mum feels the same way, so we sold up and moved here. But I don't know what it's going to be like. I didn't really want to come. It's all right for Billy, he's quite a bit older than me and already has a job as an electrician. But I've never lived in a small place like this before. Never lived in a house like this before. I've left all my friends behind and I don't know anyone here.'

And her voice wobbled just a little.

'You know me now,' I said. 'And don't worry, before very long you'll know everyone else in Auchtertuie as well, and they'll know you. It's that kind of place.'

And we chatted for ages while her mum and dad and big brother, Billy, and the removal men came and went round about us.

Finally I looked at my watch. 'I must go,' I said. 'Kirsty will be wondering where I've got to, but come over later to the Crumbling Arms and I'll introduce you to my family. They're not exactly normal either. You can't miss the inn, it's the white building facing the loch.'

Tina promised and I headed off home.

'Well,' sniffed Kirsty, as I wandered into the kitchen, 'you took your time. How was your visit?'

'Fine,' I said. 'They said thank you for the scones.'

And I stopped deliberately, just to wind her up.

'And?'

'They were delicious. I had some too.'

'And?'

'The jam was delicious as well.'

Kirsty narrowed her eyes and gave me her 'you are getting right up my nose, Kat McCrumble' look.

'And?'

'I dropped some on my sweatshirt, but you can hardly see the mark. Look. It's just a bit sticky.'

Kirsty drew a deep breath and put her hands on her hips. A warning sign.

'Oh, would you like to know what the new people are like?' I asked innocently.

Kirsty looked like she was about to burst her knicker elastic, so I took pity on her.

'Well . . . their name's Morrison. Dad is David, mum is Terri, big brother is William, known as Billy, and there's Tina who's about a month younger than me. They sold up their place in London and are going to set up in business in Auchtertuie.'

'Doing what?' asked Kirsty.

17

'David's hobby is making pots, so he's hoping to put a kiln in one of the outhouses and get a little pottery going. Terri makes things from sheep.'

'I make things from sheep,' said Kirsty. 'Lamb hotpot, Scotch broth, the occasional jumper.'

'Ah,' I said, 'but you get your meat from James Ross, the butcher, and your wool whenever you go to the wool shop in Inverness. Terri is going to get her wool direct from the sheep, or at least from the fences the wool catches on. Then she's going to dye it, spin it and make it into things.'

'I think it'd be easier to go to Inverness,' sniffed Kirsty.

'But that's not all. Do you want to hear more?'

Do children want presents at Christmas? Kirsty sat down opposite me at the kitchen table.

'More about the sheep, that is. Terri thinks sheep's heads are very beautiful.'

'Och, she'll get on well with the butcher, then.'

I shook my head. 'She's going to search the hills for bleached sheep's skulls and turn them into some kind of art. Put little tea lights in them or knit them woolly hats, I don't know.'

'Uh huh.'

Now Kirsty has several 'uh huh's. They range from uh huh meaning 'oh, all right then' to uh huh meaning 'this person is a serious lunatic and should not be allowed out alone.' Guess which one this was.

'Terri can't cook either, Tina says. So I've invited Tina over later. She thinks your scones are wonderful.'

'Och well, we'd better feed the poor wee lassie up, then, if her mother's more into crafts than casseroles. Is that it?' she added.

I searched my memory for more gossip.

'Em . . . Tina says her big brother is a bampot. Walks around making dalek noises and goes to Star Trek conventions and movies in an outfit his mum made him. Mr Spock, I think.'

'Oh well, if her brother's an idiot he'll fit in well around here. Now, if you don't mind, Kat McCrumble, I must get on with my work. Can't sit around here all day chatting to you.'

What a cheek!

Tina came round later that afternoon, once the removal men had gone and she had sorted out where she was going to sleep.

'I had the removers put my bed in the tiny room at the top of the stairs,' she said, 'and I lay down to try it out, but when I sat up, I banged my head on the sloping ceiling.' And she showed me the slight bruise on her forehead. It showed up a little bit blue on her creamy skin. Now why did no freckles land on her?

'If it gets too bad,' I told her, 'you can either move your bed or move in here. We take in most things in distress.'

Kirsty sat Tina down and gave her a large slice of apple pie. Max gave Tina a paw because he wanted a share of the pie. Millie, as usual, was polite and just snuffled up any crumbs.

Then I took Tina out to the back yard to introduce her to the rest of the animals.

'What a fantastic place, Kat,' she said. 'You're so lucky to live here. I could never have a pet in our London flat; everyone was out all day, and Mum's a bit allergic. Maybe our move up here won't be so bad after all.'

And we talked some more. Tina and I have been best friends ever since and she's shared in some of the crazy things that have happened to me in Auchtertuie . . .

Chapter 4

Today started off quite normally. Normal for the Crumbling Arms, that is. The smoke alarm announced that Dad had burnt the toast again, and I hurriedly threw on my clothes and hurtled downstairs to help with the breakfasts. Our guests were leaving early to get to Ullapool in time to catch the boat to Stornaway. They would need a good breakfast inside them. The weather forecast said the weather was to be 'unsettled' so that could mean anything from a heatwave to a blizzard, or possibly both.

Dad was having another try at the toast making. You would think anyone could make toast, wouldn't you? *Find toaster, insert bread, remove when brown*. It's not rocket science, but it's too tricky for my dad. He starts off all right, pops the bread into our ancient toaster and switches it on, but then, while he's waiting for it to brown, he sticks his nose in a book and forgets about everything else till: *EEAW EEAW EEAW*, the smoke alarm goes off and everyone gets an early morning alarm call, whether they want it or not.

I threw the bacon under the grill and blitzed the porridge in the microwave. Kirsty would have had forty fits if she'd seen me.

'Good porridge needs to be carefully stirred in a pot on the stove, Kat McCrumble,' she always told me, 'not zapped with rays from the outer darkness.'

I'm sure she was right, but our guests didn't have time to wait, and anyway Kirsty wouldn't be in till ten o'clock, and what her eye didn't see, I wouldn't get a row for.

Kirsty's a second cousin of Dad's, and does her best to keep an eye on me, since I have no mum. She died when I was little, but I keep a photo of her beside my bed and Dad often talks to me about her.

Morag keeps an eye on me too, but an even bigger eye on Dad. She really likes him, but he never notices. But then Dad never notices much. Things like carbonised toast and burnt porridge just pass him by, whereas anything to do with the pets or the wildlife, or the history of the McCrumbles, and he's immediately alert. He says it probably has to do with his brain only being developed on one side, but I think that's just an excuse for only bothering about what he's interested in. Now if I tried that excuse with my schoolwork . . . Come to think of it, it's probably the only one I haven't tried, and I'm pretty inventive. Especially when it comes to report card time. Do you know what my last one said?

'Katriona has worked reasonably well this year, but could do so much better if she really applied herself and stuck to it.'

Applied herself and stuck to it? Made me sound like superglue.

But Dad hadn't been too bad about the report, though he did say . . . 'If you really want to be a vet, Kat, you'll have to work harder.'

I know that's true, but . . .

Between us, Dad and I fed the guests and waved them off on their journey. I was just clearing the breakfast dishes from the dining room when a clatter, rattle and bang announced the arrival of Ali McAlly's taxi. How that car passes its road test is another mystery, but it's as well Ali doesn't have to pass one too. You don't need to remember to put your teeth in to drive a taxi, but wearing your glasses would help when, without them, you can't see much further than your belly button. And Ali always has his radio on at full blast because his hearing's not too good. Not that anyone can hear the radio above the noise of the taxi.

Ali got out and opened the door for his passenger.

'Dougal,' I cried, and abandoned the clearing up.

Millie and Max heard me yell and bounded to the front door ahead of me. They jumped up on Dougal like he was their long lost owner, which he was.

Dougal McDougall is even older than Ali, though he has considerably more teeth. He used to have a sheep farm up in the hills beyond Auchtertuie. When he retired and went to live with his daughter, Maisie, in Glasgow, he asked us to have Millie and Max, as a flat on the top floor of a Glasgow tenement was no place for two sheepdogs. Millie would probably have coped, but Max would have herded all the neighbours into the nearest park. We'd probably have had to visit him in doggy nick.

But Dougal was as delighted to see the dogs as they were to see him.

'Hi, Dougal,' I grinned, as the canine onslaught subsided and he rewarded them both with a couple of dog biscuits. 'It's great to see you. Are you back for a visit?'

'Just a quick one, Kat,' he smiled. 'I'm staying with my sister in Fort William for a couple of days, but I called to talk to you and your dad about a little matter you might be able to help me with.'

'Dad's in the kitchen,' I said. 'Come in and tell us all about it.'

But by the time Dougal had enquired kindly after everyone in Auchtertuie, caught up with all the gossip, said hullo to Donk and Lily, and thrown a ball a zillion times for Max, the kitchen had filled up, so he ended up telling Kirsty, Morag, Donald, Dad and me all about the little matter we might be able to help him with.

'The Glasgow zoo is closing down,' said Dougal, 'and homes have to be found for all the animals.'

'I'm sure we could have some of them here,' I said immediately.

Dougal patted my hand. 'I knew you'd say that, Kat, and there is a particular one I have in mind. My daughter, Maisie, is a keeper at the zoo, and is very fond of all the animals, but one in particular. She would adopt him if she could. Bring him home to stay, if she could, but that's just not possible. We couldn't even have Millie and Max, never mind Wilf.'

'And Wilf is a . . . ?' asked Dad.

'A little wallaby.'

'A wallaby!' I squeaked, and looked round for our animal book. We'd never had a wallaby before.

'Cutest little fellow you ever saw,' said Dougal. 'He's a little red-necked wallaby. He was born at the zoo, but unfortunately his mum died when he was tiny, so Maisie hand reared him. Got herself one of these little baby carriers you can strap on, so Wilf would have a pouch to live in. She carried him in front of her wherever she went till he was old enough to cope on his own. Maisie's very fond of him, as you can imagine, and is upset at the thought of being parted from him. That's what made me think of you. If you could have him, she'd know he'd gone to a good home.'

'Of course we'll take him,' I cried, 'won't we, Dad? It'll be great.'

'We can certainly give it a try,' said Dad, 'till we see if he settles down and is happy. This place is a bit different from a zoo. We'll have to see how he copes.'

'Ahem.' Dougal cleared his throat and looked slightly uncomfortable. 'I think it'll be more how *you'll* cope. I should warn you, he's very friendly, but not very bright. He's always getting into mischief.'

26

'He'll be no worse than Max, then,' I grinned.

'I'll tell Maisie you'll give it a go, then,' smiled Dougal. 'She'll be really pleased.' And he went off to get his paper at the little post office and to say hullo to some more old friends.

I found our animal book and looked up wallaby.

'It'll be under wobble U,' I grinned. I'd had difficulty with my Ws when I was little.

But then, Morag, who'd been sitting quietly, frowned. Her eye – the blue one it was, the other's amber – took on its faraway look.

'No, Kat,' she said in her funny, hollow, 'second sight' voice, 'I think you might find wallaby under T. Under T for trouble.'

Chapter 5

But I paid no heed, I was too excited. Dad didn't listen either. He's not really convinced by the second sight, and anyway he didn't want to let Dougal and Maisie down. To say nothing of Wilf.

'Och, what harm can a wee wallaby do,' said Kirsty. 'I used to watch *Skippy the Bush Kangaroo* on TV when I was little. He was a great wee fellow. Always helping to solve problems. Always catching the bad guys.' And she started to sing the theme tune to the programme.

Skippeeee, Skippeeee,
Skippeeee, the bush kangaroooo.
Skippeeee, Skippeeee,

Skippeeee, our friend ever true.

The rest of us covered our ears.

'I hope Wilf will be all right with us,' I said. 'He'll need to get on with all the McCrumbles, four-legged and two.'

'I don't think that will be a problem,' said Dad. 'Being brought up in a zoo, he'll be used to lots of animals and people. Anyway, we'll just take him on a trial basis to see how he gets on.'

'He shouldn't be too difficult to feed,' I said, pointing to a page in our animal book. 'It says here wallabies eat mainly leaves and grass, and we've plenty of good lush grass with all the rain we get. Save you getting out the lawnmower, Dad.'

Then everyone started talking about what it would be like to have a little wallaby around.

'Do you think we'll have to try to speak to him in an Australian accent?' said Kirsty.

'Not if he's been raised in Glasgow,' grinned Donald.

'We'll have to make a new run and a pen for him before we go to collect him,' said Dad. 'We must have everything prepared for his arrival. It'll be strange enough for the poor wee fellow, leaving his home and the people he knows.'

And we were so busy discussing where we would put Wilf – we have plenty of ground at the back of the inn – that we didn't really notice that Morag didn't join in. Didn't really notice how quiet she was. Didn't really notice her worried face.

Morag finally put down her empty mug and stood up. 'I must be getting on with my rounds now,' she said quietly. 'Thanks for the tea and the scone, Kirsty. I'll see you all later.'

'Bye, Morag,' we said, and went back to our discussion.

Only Millie caught Morag's mood, and accompanied her back out to her little red van, leaning a comforting head on her leg.

We decided on the site of Wilf's new quarters, and Dad said he would phone Dougal and arrange a suitable time for us to go to Glasgow to collect Wilf. I could hardly wait. I love living in Auchtertuie, but I like to visit other places too. I'd been to Glasgow before, one time on a school trip. We went to see the Burrell collection, named after Sir William Burrell who was a very wealthy business man. He travelled the world buying up the most amazing collection of just about everything you can think of: furniture, paintings, ancient pots. I liked thinking about the people who might have used these things. Imagining what they must have been like. Wondering if any of them were like me. The boys in my class loved the suits of armour and the weapons best; I preferred the old costumes. They would be really great for Hallowe'en. Save me racking my brains trying to think of a suitable outfit to get dressed up in.

Actually the best bit of the school trip was the journey home on the bus. I was lustily singing all the latest pop songs with the rest of my class, while the Nisbet boys guzzled huge bars of chocolate and fizzy Coke. Not a good idea when you're travelling on very twisty roads. The boys felt sick and stood up to ask the bus driver to stop and let them off. But they didn't make it. They threw up all over our teacher's new shoes. She wasn't pleased, and our class was never allowed away on a trip again. Funny that.

I jumped up from the kitchen table. 'I must go and tell the rest of the animals we're having a wallaby to stay,' I said. But, before I could do that, the phone rang.

'The Crumbling Arms inn,' I said. 'Kat McCrumble speaking. How may I help you?'

You have to be really polite when you run an inn, Dad says. Even when people are pains in the neck. Especially when people are pains in the neck.

' 'Allo 'allo,' said the voice at the other end. 'Vous êtes la Kat McCrumble avec les cheveux rouge?'

31

'Pardon? Yes. I mean oui,' I said, fingering my red hair.

'Vous êtes la Kat McCrumble qui a beaucoup d'animaux?'

'Er . . . oui. We have lots of animals. Er . . . who is this? Er . . . qui est-ce?' I knew I should have listened harder in the French class.

'Moi, je m'appelle Christina, mais mes amis m'appellent—'

'Tina,' I yelled. 'You're back. How was the caravanning with your cousins? How was France? I see you've been practising your French.'

'Not really,' laughed Tina. 'All the French kids I met wanted me to speak English so they could improve theirs. But I did manage to speak enough French to purchase for you un petit cadeau.'

'A little present,' I said. I understood that all right. 'Great. Thank you.'

'Why don't you come over and collect it,' said Tina, 'if you're not too busy? We can catch up with all the news.'

'I'll come tout de suite,' I said. 'I've got lots to tell you . . .'

Chapter 6

Tina had lots to tell me too. She had been on a caravan holiday in France with her aunt and uncle and some cousins. Her mum and dad's craft business is busiest in the summer so they have to stay home then.

Mrs Morrison was in the shop when I went in. They call it a shop, but really it's a kind of lean-to greenhouse tacked on to the side of their cottage. It has shelves going all the way round and is full of Mr Morrison's pots. Some look like ordinary flowerpots, some look like ordinary serving dishes, but others look like I don't know what. They're strange fantastical shapes, and you certainly couldn't put anything in them or use them for much.

'These pots are just themselves, Kat,' Mr Morrison once told me. 'Sometimes I put the clay on the wheel and the clay takes over. The pots just shape themselves.'

Aha. I had tried that once in school. I put my clay on the wheel and hit the foot pedal with enthusiasm. Sure enough the pot did shape itself. All over me and all round the craft room walls. I was only allowed to make coil pots after that. Pity. I just felt I was getting the hang of it too.

But Mr Morrison was explaining more about his odd pots.

'They're not *for* anything, Kat. They just *are*. They are things of beauty. They exist in their own right. Do you see?'

'Oh yes,' I said, lying. But it was just a little white lie. You can't tell your best friend's dad you think he's a bampot.

In among the pots were Mrs Morrison's woolly things. Using natural plant dyes, she had dyed the sheep's wool she'd collected and made it into little purses and mittens and scarves. Some of them were quite pretty. But you couldn't say that for the bleached sheep's heads she had on display. They sat mournfully on a ledge, and, when I arrived, Mrs Morrison was busy dusting them and arranging wild flowers round their horns. They still didn't look very appealing.

'Hullo, Kat,' she greeted me. 'Come to buy a sheep's head? They're going cheap today.'

'Shouldn't that be going *baa*?' I grinned, and wandered into the house to look for Tina. She was in the kitchen, stuffing her holiday laundry into the ancient washing-machine. Mrs Morrison doesn't worry overmuch about cleanliness. Tina does. She's as tidy as her mum's untidy. Funny that. Or maybe not. Kirsty is always on at me for being so scruffy. Always on at me to smarten up. But I like scruffy. It's comfortable. Anyway you can't worry too much about clothes when you're around animals all day.

'Hi, Kat,' said Tina, and hugged me, which considering I probably smelt of donkey doo was a sign of true friendship. 'Great to see you.'

'You too,' I grinned.

'Come upstairs to my room,' said Tina. 'Your pressie's there. I hope you like it.'

We trooped upstairs to Tina's tiny bedroom. Like Tina, it was neat and tidy. Everything was where it should be. Her books were in the bookcase – mine litter the floor. The cuddly toys she can't bear to part with peered at us from the top of the wardrobe – mine still vie with me for space in my bed, and, speaking of which, Tina's was neatly made. Mine – well you can guess.

Sitting on Tina's bed was a little parcel.

'This is for you,' she said, handing it to me.

'Wow!' I said. 'It looks almost too good to open.' And it did. It was a small, pale blue, rectangular parcel with a fancy gold shop label at one end. From the label hung a scrunch of shiny yellow ribbons. Neat.

'Go on, open it,' said Tina.

I opened the parcel carefully and drew out the prettiest beaded bracelet. The beads were multicoloured and sparkled in the sun streaming through the tiny attic window.

'It's lovely,' I said, putting it on. 'Thank you very much, Tina.'

Tina smiled. 'I had to bring everyone something small that wouldn't take up too much space in the caravan. I brought Mum a pretty ceramic soap dish with holes in the bottom. She thought it might be for straining individual portions of peas.'

'She's not really into soap, is she?' I grinned. 'But tell me all about your holiday. Did you meet any nice French boys?'

'Oh, Kat,' she blushed.

'What's his name?'

'Marc.'

'OK. You tell me all about Marc and I'll tell you all about Archie. He's an American McCrumble who was recently staying at the Crumbling Arms. We're keeping in touch.'

And we spent so long catching up with each other's news that Mrs Morrison invited me to stay for lunch. I opened my mouth, but couldn't come up with a good excuse. Fortunately, Tina came to my rescue.

'Actually, Mum, Kat's already asked me to go to her place.'

It was only a little white lie. I had been going to ask her.

'Fine.' Mrs Morrison smiled vaguely. 'I don't know what we're having anyway. There might be some of last night's stew left, I suppose.'

'There's practically all of it left,' whispered Tina, making vomiting motions to me behind her mum's back. 'No one could eat it.'

We hurried back to the Crumbling Arms to see what Kirsty had made for lunch.

'Oh, Kirsty,' said Tina when we entered the kitchen. 'What a lovely smell. Is it shepherd's pie?'

'It is indeed,' said Kirsty, and pulled out a chair for Tina to sit down at the table.

'It's one of my favourites,' sighed Tina.

'Och, and here's me thinking you would be

37

coming back from France with fancy ideas about eating snails and frogs' legs, and turning up your nose at mince and tatties.'

'Never,' said Tina. 'The French food was good. It was just different and . . .'

'There's nothing like what you get at home,' smiled Kirsty.

'*This* is nothing like what I get at home,' said Tina, and told Kirsty about the stew.

'Dearie me,' said Kirsty, piling up Tina's plate with the steaming shepherd's pie. 'Still, perhaps you can't be arty-crafty *and* a good cook. Everyone has a different talent.'

'Oh,' I said. 'I wonder what mine is?'

'Getting mad, being scruffy, creating havoc . . .' Kirsty had quite a list.

But, for once, I didn't bother to reply. My mouth was far too full.

Chapter 7

I said I'd tell you more about Old Hamish, our ghost, didn't I? Well, if I sound very matter-of-fact about him, it's because he doesn't scare me now. He did the first time I saw him; I let out a yell you could have heard on the other side of the moon. But now I know he doesn't mean me any harm, quite the reverse. He usually appears in the Crumbling Arms when there's a problem, and I know he tries to help. But Dad's not convinced he exists at all, so we usually agree to disagree about Old Hamish.

You see, long ago, in the misty, murky past, there was a McCrumble castle with lots of land round about. The castle and the land were owned by twin brothers Hamish and Callum. But they couldn't have been less alike. Hamish was hard working and did his best to look after the castle, the land and the people on it. Callum didn't care what happened to any of it, he just wanted to spend all the money on himself. Which he did, before he took off and disappeared. He left Hamish with lots of debts. Hamish worked hard to try to pay them off. He wanted to keep the McCrumble good name. That meant there was no money left over to repair the castle, which eventually fell into ruin.

Many years later another McCrumble used the stones of the old castle to build the Crumbling Arms inn and there's been a McCrumble there ever since.

Everyone in Auchtertuie knows the story of Old Hamish and everyone believes I have seen him, except Dad. He's still sceptical about ghosts. Good thing the Nisbet boys aren't.

When Tina had gone back home to do the rest of her laundry, I had a word with the pets about our impending new arrival. I went into the back yard with Millie and Max and sat on an upturned bucket by Donk and Lily's pen. Donk and Lily immediately ambled over to see me. Was this because of my scintillating conversation? Was it because of my sparkling personality? Nope. They probably reckoned I had pinched some of Kirsty's carrots for them, which I had. I also had some doggy chocs in my pocket. Max can smell them at a hundred metres so his nose was as far into my pocket as it could go.

'Sit,' I told him.

Millie sat, Max kept on snuffling.

I went into my other pocket and offered him a carrot.

He gave me his 'you must be joking' look, followed by his 'you know I'm a serious chocoholic' look, followed by his 'don't you know it's not nice to tease dumb animals?' look, followed by a paw. He knew that never failed. He was right, and while I fed the pets their treats I told them about Wilf.

'We're going to have someone new to stay with us soon,' I said. 'A new animal. A different kind from any you've met before. This one doesn't eat carrots or chocolate, as far as I know, so you don't need to worry about that.'

I looked round at them all. No one seemed in the least worried. Donk was giving a toothy yawn which Lily immediately copied. Millie had sat down beside me and half closed her eyes against the bright sunlight, and Max was playing football with a beetle that had foolishly crept out from underneath my bucket.

'There's going to be a bit of hammering and

banging for a while till we make a new home for Wilf. Did I tell you he's a wallaby?'

By now, Donk and Lily were scratching their necks on the fence post, Millie's eyes were reduced to slits, and Max had decided the beetle was no fun and had resorted to chasing his tail.

But I pressed on with their education. 'Wallabies are from Australia, you know, except this one's from Glasgow. He's used to living in a zoo, but we're hoping he'll like living with us. Dad and I will have to go to Glasgow to fetch him, but Kirsty and Donald will look after you. You won't fret, will you?' I said, to their retreating backs. Apparently not.

The only pet I hadn't told was Samantha, and she just wasn't around. She'd probably be up a tree somewhere, observing us all.

I got up from my bucket and saw Dad and Donald approaching, carrying long planks of wood.

'There you are, Kat,' said Dad. 'Fetch the hammer and nails and you can lend a hand.' Now do you see why I'm generally so scruffy!

We chose a patch of ground not too far away from the inn and adjoining Donk and Lily's pen. We hoped the donkeys and the wallaby would be company for each other and get to be friends.

Before too long, under Donald's excellent guidance, Wilf's new home began to take shape. It wouldn't be elegant, but we hoped Wilf would be comfortable. All we had to do now was go and get him.

Meantime there was some other news.

As often happened, Morag got wind of it first. She came in that evening to give Kirsty a hand in the kitchen, as she often does when we're busy. It has a little to do with Morag and Kirsty being friends, and a lot to do with Morag fancying Dad.

I was bringing through the empty pudding plates from the dining room – everyone had had double helpings of cranachan and was now waiting for their coffee and delicious chunks of Kirsty's tablet – when Morag had one of her 'turns'. She stiffened and her eyes took on their faraway look. Fortunately, Kirsty noticed and rescued the glass Morag was drying at the time.

Kirsty put a chair behind Morag and pushed her gently into it. Morag's voice came out as though it belonged to someone far away . . .

'Auchtertuie's very busy . . .'

'Och, it's always busy at this time of year,' said Kirsty.

Morag carried on . . .

'An enormous car. A long, long car. A white car . . .'

'There'll be something on at the big hotel on the

estate. There's always comings and goings there. It'll be some bigwig or other in his stretch limo.' Kirsty was dismissive. She didn't like the hotel or its owners C.P. Associates, whoever *they* were. The hotel had played some dirty tricks on us in the recent past and had tried to close us down, and turn the inn into a tartan centre, which would make them money. We'd outwitted them so far, but still couldn't prove anything against them. Despite the best efforts of Constable Ross, our local policeman, C.P. Associates were still a mystery, though we knew someone was ordering the horrible gamekeeper, Ron Jackson, to harass us as much as possible and drive us out.

But we were still here.

So was Morag.

'Such a lot of excitement,' she said, in that same odd voice.

'Flashlights popping.' She started back and closed her eyes as if against their glare. 'And big crowds outside the Crumbling Arms . . .'

Then she stopped abruptly and came out of her trance.

'Oh,' she said, giving herself a little shake. 'What did I say?'

'Nothing that makes a lot of sense at the moment.' Kirsty patted Morag's hand. 'Perhaps later . . .'

Certainly later as it turned out.

Chapter 8

A couple of days later Dad and I set off in our old van for Glasgow. We use the van for everything: going on picnics, collecting logs for the fire, transporting animals when necessary. Now we were going to collect Wilf. Dad had had a long telephone conversation with Maisie. She was obviously pleased we were going to look after Wilf, but was really sad to lose him. I hoped he wouldn't mind being bumped about a bit in the back of our old van. Dad and Donald had fitted dog guards into the back to keep Wilf as safe as possible, and I had put in some fresh grass and some old blankets in case he felt like a snooze. I'd also put in an ancient teddy of mine that I'd grown out of. (Well, I hadn't really grown out of it, but I thought Wilf might need it more than me.)

We left very early in the morning with only Samantha, returning home from one of her nocturnal jaunts, to see us off.

'We'll be back soon with a little wallaby called Wilf,' I told her.

Samantha gave me her 'are you speaking to me?' look, followed by her 'and what makes you think I'd be interested anyway?' look, and flicked her tail before making her way in through the cat flap.

'I'll miss you too,' I called after her, but she paid no heed.

Dad drove at a steady pace, mindful of the wildlife that might be on its way home in the early morning. A fox, jogging by the side of the road, gave us a startled look and shot off, affording us a brief glimpse of his bushy tail. A couple of male pheasants wandered across the road in front of us. They're large, brilliantly coloured birds with magnificent long tails and very few brains. They gave us a curious look, then ran zigzagging across the road before finally deciding which way was best. The fields were full of rabbits having an early morning munch, and a solitary barn owl sat on a fence post, eyeing them up. But they were too big to be his breakfast. The morning air was full of birdsong as a thin mist rose from the loch and evaporated in the sunshine.

I sighed happily. I loved the wildlife. I loved Auchtertuie and wouldn't want to live anywhere else, but a trip to Glasgow to collect a wallaby was something different.

'Are we going straight to the zoo?' I asked.

Dad nodded. 'Dougal will meet us there and show us where to find Maisie and Wilf.'

I could hardly wait.

We crossed over the bridge at Ballahulich – easier to say than you think, try Ba-la-hool-ish – and headed for Glencoe. I've been to Glencoe lots of times, but I still find it an eerie place. It's a ten-mile-long pass among the mountains and runs to the sea at Loch Leven. It's a beautiful, wild place, but in 1692 the MacDonalds of Glencoe were massacred there by the Campbells. It's said Glencoe means the Glen of Weeping. I expect you can see why. Then we headed over Rannoch moor. Lovely in summer, bleak in winter. After that it was past Crianlarich – Cree-an-lar-ich (see, you're getting good now) – and along Loch Lomondside. This is now part of Scotland's first national park and is beautiful. Well, I would say that, wouldn't I?

Finally we hit the busy roads around Glasgow. Dad had phoned ahead to give Dougal our estimated time of arrival and he was there waiting for us when we drew up outside the zoo. Dougal showed us to a back entrance, then took us to meet Maisie and Wilf.

Maisie looked like Dougal. Much younger, of course, and a lot less craggy, but she had his same broad smile and softly spoken voice. At her side, hanging on to her trouser leg, was a little wallaby.

'Meet Wilf,' grinned Maisie.

I hunkered down and took out some of the grass I had stuffed into my pocket. I held it out to him. Wilf looked at it, looked at me and came to a decision. He grabbed the grass with both hands and stuffed it into his mouth. Then he had a rummage in my pocket to see if there was any more.

'He likes you, Kat,' said Maisie. 'I can tell.'

I liked him too. He was the first red-necked wallaby I'd seen up close. He was about the size of a biggish dog, with an extra-long tail – a fawny grey colour with a reddish nape and shoulders. Officially, I discovered, his name is *Macropus rufogriseus*. And I have the cheek to complain about my full name!

We chatted to Maisie and I played a game of 'I bet I can jump further than you' with Wilf. Wilf won easily.

Finally, Maisie said, 'Well, what do you think?

Would he fit into your set-up at the Crumbling Arms? As you can see, he's a lively wee chap and will get into any mischief that he can. He's used to a lot of attention, so I need to find him a good home with people he likes and that like him.'

Dad and I looked at each other. Wilf was scratching at my leg and wanted me to follow him round his enclosure.

'I think we can offer him a good home,' said Dad, 'but it's really up to Wilf. Let's have him for a little while to see if he settles. We'll keep in touch to let you know how he's getting on.'

'Fine,' said Maisie. 'The only thing I should warn you about is not to give him too much fruit to eat. He absolutely loves it, but it gives him terrible tummy ache.' Then she went to get Wilf ready for his big journey north.

'It'll be a weight off her mind if he stays with you,' said Dougal. 'She's been worried for weeks now about what will happen to Wilf when the zoo closes down.'

Maisie came back carrying some of Wilf's favourite oak leaves, then she helped settle him in the back of the van. It was a tearful Maisie who waved him goodbye outside the Glasgow zoo. Wilf watched her through the window of the van till we turned the corner and she was out of sight.

'Gosh,' I said to Dad as we headed round the north of Glasgow towards Loch Lomond again. 'A little wallaby. We've never looked after a wallaby before.'

'No,' said Dad. 'He'll take a bit of getting used to, but he's a cute little fellow, I'm sure he'll be no trouble.'

Trouble? Now where had I heard that word before? Ah, didn't Morag say something about Wilf and trouble?

Oh no, I thought to myself, Morag must have got it wrong. How could a wee chap like Wilf bring anybody any trouble?

How idiotic can one girl be?

Chapter 9

Wilf looked out of the window at the passing scenery for a little while then explored the interior of the van. He nibbled some of the grass, poked about in the blankets and found my old teddy. He gave it a sniff, but decided it wasn't for eating and dropped it. Then he came up towards our end of the van.

'Hullo, Wilf,' I said.

In reply, Wilf reached through the dog guard with both little paws and yanked my hair.

'Ow!' The yell made Dad swerve, and he nearly ran into the back of a lorry slowing down for some roadworks.

'Sorry, Dad,' I gasped. 'Wilf pulled my hair. I

don't know if he's seen red hair up so close before.'

Wilf reached through the bars again. This hair pulling was going to be a good game. I'd have none left by the time we got to Auchtertuie.

'Oh no, you don't, Wilf,' I said, and rummaged in the glove compartment for a hat to wear. I was hoping for the old ski hat Dad sometimes kept there. What I found was the hat I'd worn to the Morrisons' fancy dress party at Christmas time. It was made of bright green velvet and had large brown flashing antlers. I had only worn it as a joke – now the joke was on me. But I had no choice. I put it on and tucked my hair up underneath. Small children stared at me and pointed, lorry drivers laughed and gave me the thumbs-up sign, and people in passing cars thought Christmas had come early. My face turned as red as my hair.

'Cool hat, Kat,' smiled Dad.

We stopped briefly on Loch Lomondside to eat the packed lunch Kirsty had made up.

'I wonder if we'll see any of Wilf's friends here,' I said to Dad, who was busy fastening a soft dog collar round Wilf's neck. 'I discovered that there used to be a colony of red-necked wallabies on one of the larger islands on Loch Lomond, and, in severe winters, some would hop across the frozen loch to live in the woodlands at the lochside.'

'I didn't know that,' said Dad.

'Neither did I till I started to find out all about wallabies.'

We let Wilf out of the van on an extending lead. He was fine while I gave him some fresh leaves, but then he decided to explore. That's when I found out how quickly a wallaby can hop. And, it was a mistake to decide to eat our lunch by some pine trees. Wilf found the trees fascinating. Round and round them he went. Round and round them the lead went. Round and round them I went after him.

Other people were picnicking at the same spot. They were delighted by Wilf's antics. Wilf realised this and played up even more. He pinched a little boy's ball, sniffed it and dropped it. It rolled into the loch. The child started to yell.

'I'm sorry,' I panted to the mother. 'Wilf can be a bit mischievous, and I don't have another ball to give you.'

The child wailed louder than ever and pointed at my head. 'Want that. Want that.'

It was only then I realised I was still wearing the Rudolph hat. I took it off and gave it to him. He was welcome to it.

We put Wilf back into the van before he could cause any more trouble and set off for home. Wilf, tired out from his antics, settled down to sleep.

Thank goodness; I was worn out and we were nowhere near Auchtertuie yet.

Finally we reached the Crumbling Arms. The journey had been a slow one as we'd got stuck in tourist traffic. Dad couldn't drive fast anyway with Wilf in the back. As we came along the shore road, we could see a reception committee outside the Crumbling Arms, waiting to greet us. Kirsty, Morag and Donald couldn't wait to see Wilf. Neither could half of Auchtertuie, who had all heard about our new arrival. Jinty McCrumble from the bakery was there, as well as Lachy McCrumble, in from his boat on the loch. Luigi McCrumble from the Auchtertuie chippy had deserted his deep fat fryer and battered haddock to come and have a look. Even Constable Ross, Willie to his friends when he was off duty, had come to inspect Wilf.

'Oh,' I said to Dad, when I saw the crowd. 'Do you think Wilf might be upset with all these people looking at him?'

'Shouldn't think so,' said Dad. 'He used to be in a zoo, remember.'

We got Wilf out from the back of the van and he looked at the crowd. Then he preened himself like a movie star. What a show-off! He'd have signed autographs if he could. He wasn't at all upset by the attention, he loved it.

Once he had been suitably admired, we took him into the Crumbling Arms and introduced him to the pets. Millie gave Wilf a ladylike sniff and wagged her tail. Max ran round and round him, barking excitedly, his tail waving like a flag in the wind. Wilf wasn't bothered at all. He had obviously encountered daft dogs before.

'Quiet, Max,' I said.

He ignored me.

'Quiet, Max,' said Dad.

He ignored Dad.

Wilf thwacked his tail on the kitchen floor. It made an impressive noise. Max stopped barking and went to investigate Wilf's tail. He'd never heard one that loud before, or seen one that long before. He decided there and then that Wilf was a pal, and soon the three animals were playing chases round the kitchen table.

'Right,' said Kirsty, 'if you'll just sort out these creatures, I'll see about some food.'

'There's a great smell coming from the oven, Kirsty,' I said. Suddenly I realised how hungry I was. Suddenly I realised I'd completely forgotten to eat my lunch because of Wilf's antics by the lochside.

'It's slow cooked beef casserole,' said Kirsty. 'I wasn't sure what time you'd be home. And there's enough for everyone,' she added, looking round at the small crowd we still had with us.

Accompanied by Millie and Max, we took Wilf out to his pen. Donk and Lily looked over interestedly. Donk gave a nod which Lily immediately copied. Wilf thumped his tail in hullo, and that was that. Wilf was accepted.

We showed Wilf to his little house, gave him plenty of fresh grass and leaves and left him to it. He'd had a busy day. Millie stood guard over him for a little while then followed us back indoors.

Max was already there. Wilf might be his new pal, but there was food to be had and slow cooked beef casserole was Max's favourite, along with everything else Kirsty made. Morag had laid several places at the table and a variety of McCrumbles sat down, but only one Ross. Constable Ross, son of James Ross, the butcher. Constable Ross took off his policeman's hat and metamorphosed into Willie. We were halfway through the beef in its rich brown gravy when Willie said, 'I have some news.'

Every knife and fork at the table went down and faces turned expectantly to Willie.

'It's not official yet, so I'll ask you to keep it to yourselves for a few days.' And he looked at everyone and grinned. He knew that keeping secrets in Auchtertuie was almost impossible.

Everyone nodded, 'Oh yes, oh yes,' anyway.

'Well,' said Willie, drawing out the suspense. 'You know the big hotel on the estate.'

Of course we did.

'Well you know how it quite often has a famous guest.'

Of course we did.

'Well . . .' Willie was enjoying being the centre of attention. 'They're having another. Or, at least, several others, I suppose.'

'Who?' I asked.

'Abandon Hope.'

'Abandon Hope!' I squeaked.

'Who are they?' asked Dad.

'Oh, Dad,' I said.

'Oh, Hector,' said Kirsty and Morag.

'Oh, help,' said Jinty. 'Even I've heard of them.'

'And me,' said Lachy. 'They're not too bad. I sometimes listen to them on the radio when I'm out on my boat.'

'Who?' said Dad again.

'A band,' I said. 'They're a famous band.'

'Oh, a pop group,' said Dad.

'Not just a *pop group*,' I said. 'They're fantastic, they're incredible, they're cutting edge, they're . . .'

'Seriously cute,' giggled Kirsty.

'That too,' I grinned. 'And they're coming to stay at the big hotel soon, Willie?'

Willie Ross nodded. 'Not sure just when yet, but they want a bit of peace and quiet after their big tour. But, remember, Kat. It's a secret.'

Yeah right! I couldn't wait to tell Tina. She was their second biggest fan. Guess who was their first.

I sneaked away to phone Tina as soon as Willie Ross had left.

'Hi,' she said. 'You're back. How is Wilf? I wanted to come over to see him, but my relatives arrived with the photos from our holiday in France and I couldn't get away.'

'Come over first thing in the morning then and see Wilf.' Then I paused and copied Willie Ross's tactics. 'Do you remember when you first came here, Tina, how you wondered if you'd like Auchtertuie? You thought it was going to be so quiet compared to London.'

'Uh huh.'

'Do you remember how you thought probably nothing ever happened?'

'Uh huh.'

'Well, something has happened.'

'You mean about Wilf arriving.'

'No, something else. I have big BIG news.'

'Tell me.'

'It's supposed to be a secret. Perhaps I'll tell you tomorrow.'

'You can be so maddening, Kat McCrumble. Tell me now.'

'OK,' I grinned. 'Guess who's coming to stay at the big hotel on the estate.'

'Don't know.'

'Only Abandon Hope.'

I could probably have heard her screech without my mobile phone.

'You're joking.'

'I never joke about anything as serious as this.'

'Wow!' said Tina. 'Wow!'

I couldn't have put it better myself.

Chapter 10

I could hardly get to sleep that night for thinking about all that had happened. What a day it had been. First there was Wilf. He was such a friendly wee fellow, but would he miss the zoo and Maisie? Would he settle down with us and the other animals? Would he like his new home? Despite his attraction to my red hair, I thought he was really cute and was looking forward to having him around. I really didn't think he'd be any trouble at all. Then there was Abandon Hope. I could hardly believe they were really coming to Auchtertuie. Tina and I had often talked about going to one of their concerts in Glasgow or Edinburgh, but we'd never had enough money, so we'd had to be content with watching them on the telly. But now they were going to be so close to us, living in the big hotel on the estate, we just had to see them. Imagine if they drove up in one of those limos with the tinted windows and disappeared into the hotel, and we didn't even catch a glimpse of them. That would be terrible. We would probably never be so close to them again!

Eventually, I fell asleep and had the strangest dream. I was at an Abandon Hope concert and they were playing their latest hit single. I was singing along with them, having a great time, when things began to change. Instead of the usual line-up of Micky (my favourite), Smart, Dev, Pete and Chris, their places were taken by Millie, Max, Wilf, Donk and Lily. Millie, Donk and Lily were in the background playing their guitars while Max and Wilf were up front, clowning around and getting all the attention. I was wearing the Rudolph hat and dancing with Tina. Her big brother, Billy, and the Nisbet boys were dancing too. Then an alarm sounded.

'Help!' I shouted. 'Fire, everyone out. Everyone out!'

I sat bolt upright in bed and wakened up Max – who frequently sneaked up on to my duvet in the night – then jumped out of bed and tripped over Millie – who didn't.

'Fire. Everyone out,' I yelled again.

Max ignored me and crawled into the warm space I had left. Millie gave me her patient look. The one that says, 'Calm down, Kat. It's only the smoke alarm. It goes off most mornings. You know it only means your dad has burnt the toast again. I can hear him scraping the black bits off from here.'

I took a deep breath, wakened up properly and calmed down.

'Sorry, guys,' I grinned. 'Strange dream.' And I told them they'd been in it, and I told them the news about Abandon Hope. Of course, I swore them to secrecy.

I needn't have bothered; everyone in Auchtertuie now knew all about it. Thanks to Morag. Dad teased her when she brought in our mail and sat down at the kitchen table to have her usual cup of tea.

'I'm surprised at you, Morag,' he grinned. 'Stupendous news about Abandon Hope coming to stay nearby, and we have to hear about it from Willie Ross. I'm surprised you didn't forewarn us. I'm surprised you didn't "see" anything about it.'

Morag harumphed through a mouthful of tattie scone.

'Don't mind him, Morag,' I said. 'He didn't even know who Abandon Hope were until last night.'

'True,' laughed Dad, and left to check the

temperature of the radiators in one of the upstairs bedrooms.

'We're expecting a guest,' I told Morag. 'Another McCrumble. Robert McCrumble Swift from the Gold Coast in Australia. He's reserved a room till the end of the month as he's not exactly sure when he'll arrive.'

Morag wasn't surprised. We get McCrumbles coming to us from all over the world, curious to see where their ancestors came from, and Dad just loves to talk to them about the family history.

'Perhaps Robert McCrumble Swift will know all about wallabies,' I said. 'And we can introduce him to Wilf.'

'Ah, Wilf,' said Morag, and her blue eye took on its faraway look.

'What is it, Morag?' I said. 'You're not still worried about Wilf.'

'I see . . . trouble,' said Morag. 'I see Wilf and . . . trouble.' And she came back to me looking anxious. 'I have a feeling about Wilf, Kat,' she said. 'It's not a good feeling. I can't explain it. It just feels like . . . trouble. Where is he now?'

'Out in his pen,' I said. 'I saw him from my bedroom window earlier, chatting to Donk and Lily. I'm going to take him out some fresh grass now. Come and say hullo.'

Morag came out to the back yard with me. Millie and Max ran on ahead. Max immediately bounded up to Wilf and they greeted each other like long lost brothers. I opened the door of Wilf's pen and he came out into the yard. He took the grass I offered then he and Max played a game of hopping and leaping.

'See?' I said to Morag. 'Look how well Wilf's fitted in already. I think he's going to be all right. I don't think there will be any trouble.'

But Morag wasn't convinced. 'I don't know,' she frowned. 'There's just something . . . it's on the edge of my mind and I can't quite reach it.'

Then she turned on her heel. 'I must get on with my round now, Kat. I'll see you later.'

Millie watched her go, then ran after her. She pressed a comforting head on Morag's leg. Morag smiled and patted her. I frowned, then shrugged my shoulders. Wilf would be fine. Even Morag could get things wrong sometimes.

Anyway, I had other things to think about. Abandon Hope were going to be living nearby and I was determined to get to see them. The only problem was how.

Chapter 11

Tina came over as soon as she could. I was still helping to serve breakfast to the guests, so she lent a hand.

Funnily enough, we had a family staying with us who lived not far away from Tina's old home in London. They were called Hobson and were touring the Highlands. Of course, they recognised her accent and got chatting.

'How do you like living here?' they asked her.

'Well . . .' Tina was truthful. 'I didn't want to come at all. I thought Mum and Dad were taking me to the far end of the earth. I knew I would miss my friends and I thought I would never make any new ones. But I did and now I like it. There's so much to do.' And she told them all about the wildlife: the golden eagles, the red deer, the red squirrels, the badgers – and *our* badger, Flip. She told them about the walks and the fishing. She even told them about the Auchtertuie Highland Games which were due to be held soon. 'Perhaps you could look in on them on your way back home,' she said. 'They're great fun.'

The Hobsons promised to try.

'You're better than a tourist guide,' I whispered to her on my way past. 'Now that's the last of the dishes cleared. Come outside and meet Wilf.'

Tina loved Wilf. She had seen lots of wallabies at Whipsnade zoo when she was little, but not one as friendly as Wilf. She tickled his white chest and stroked his fawny grey coat.

'Female wallabies are called fliers or jills and males are called boomers or jacks,' I told her, airing my new-found knowledge.

Tina just nodded; she was used to me being Little Miss Knowalot about animals. She was also used to me being Miss Knowverylittle at times in school.

Then we got down to the serious business of discussing Abandon Hope. We discussed Micky's cutting-edge hairstyle while we groomed Donk and Lily. We discussed Smart's high IQ while we played with Wilf and Millie and Max. We even told

Samantha, when she strolled by, that Abandon Hope were going to be in the area, but she flicked her tail and pretended not to be impressed. We went back indoors and told anyone who would listen how handsome all the boys were. Kirsty agreed with us, but Donald, tacking on a bit of pipe that had come adrift from a wall in the kitchen, stopped mid-hammer to enquire . . .

'More good-looking than me, you mean?'

'Er . . . you're the best-looking druid we know, Donald,' I said. Diplomatic or what?

Donald just grinned and resumed his hammering.

When Tina and I had exhausted how talented, well dressed and generally scrummy the band was, we got down to the really serious problem of how we were going to get to see them.

'Perhaps they'll come into the Crumbling Arms for a drink,' said Tina.

'Perhaps they'll come into your shop for a flowerpot or a sheep's head,' I said.

But we both thought these situations were unlikely.

'But they might pop into the post office for some stamps,' I said. 'Or to send "Greetings from Auchtertuie" postcards to their mums.'

'Or they might go into Jinty's bakery for a cup of tea and a scone.'

But we really knew that these situations were unlikely too.

'All these things are bound to be available at the big hotel,' sighed Tina. 'And they're coming here for a rest, to get away from the crowds.'

'Then there's only one thing for it,' I said. 'If they don't come to see us, we'll have to go and see them.'

'How?' said Tina. 'We can't just march up to the front door of the hotel and say, "Excuse me, we're big fans of Abandon Hope, can we speak to them, please?" Even if we got anywhere near the front door, they'd chase us for our lives.'

'Hmm,' I said. 'If the band are coming here for a rest after their big tour, they'll probably want to chill out and take things easy. Laze about, have a swim, go for walks on the estate, etc.'

'Sure to,' said Tina.

'Then we could go for walks on the estate too,' I said. 'Who knows, we might even bump into them?'

'But we'd never be allowed,' said Tina. 'C.P. Associates would never give us permission to go on to the estate.'

'Who said anything about permission?'

'Oh,' said Tina. 'You mean . . .'

'Sneak in. I know the estate almost as well as Donald does. I know lots of good places to hide. It would be easy.'

'But what if we got caught by that rotten gamekeeper? Ron Jackson's a nasty piece of work. He bought one of Dad's pots the other day then brought it back because he said it was cracked. But it wasn't cracked when he bought it. Dad always checks very carefully. We reckon Ron Jackson probably dropped it himself. I don't like him.'

'No one does,' I agreed. 'But we can stay well out of his way. What do you think? Shall we do it?'

'It's still a bit of a risk,' said Tina, who was very law-abiding.

'There's no law of trespass in Scotland,' I told her, 'and unless we were bent on doing some harm to the estate, which we're not . . .'

Tina still looked a bit worried.

'We might just get to see Abandon Hope. Might just get an autograph. Might even get our photos taken with them . . .'

That did it.

'OK,' she grinned. 'Let's do it. But how will we know when they've arrived? So many limos with tinted windows go up that long drive to the hotel, and there could be anybody in them. We don't want to risk going into the estate just to bump into some stuffy old politician.'

'Morag,' I replied. 'She knows everybody and all the gossip there is to know. She'll let us know.'

'Hmm.' Tina was doubtful. 'She didn't know Abandon Hope were coming.'

'No, she had her mind on other things. But she does know Henry McCrumble's wife, Lottie's second cousin, Sarah.'

'And?'

'She's a waitress at the big hotel.'

'Aha,' said Tina.

'Aha,' I agreed. 'Look out your camera and your autograph book.'

Tina grinned and we settled down to plan our various 'walks' through the estate. But the trouble with plans is they don't always work out. As our national poet, Robert Burns, once wrote, 'The best laid schemes of mice and men gang aft agley.'

I couldn't have put it better myself.

Chapter 12

Abandon Hope had a big rival in the stardom stakes: Wilf. It didn't take him long to work out that he liked us and liked his new home. He decided to take his rightful place in Auchtertuie and become its main tourist attraction. Never mind the magnificent, sometimes dangerous, Ben Bracken with its darkly coniferous lower slopes and its snowy peak. Never mind the mysterious, sometimes dangerous, Loch Bracken with its unfathomed depths and its scary sea monster. (Actually there isn't one. Lachy McCrumble just made that up to tempt tourists out on his boat. I *think*!) Never mind the abundant wildlife, the red squirrels, red deer, golden eagles, etc. What were these attractions compared to a cheeky wee wallaby who was a limelight case and everybody's friend?

We soon found out that the pen we had so carefully built for him was not Wilf-proof. We discovered it first when we found him in the kitchen one morning with half the contents of Kirsty's larder on the floor. He wasn't eating, just investigating. Max was investigating *and* eating. Trouble was Max didn't know when to stop eating, and, when Kirsty came back from her shopping, she found Wilf raiding her larder and Max throwing up in a corner. Kirsty was not happy. You could have heard her yell from the top of Ben Bracken. I certainly heard it in my bedroom, even above the sound of Abandon Hope, which I was playing at full blast because I knew the inn was empty. I was just in the middle of working out a fantastic dance routine that Tina and I could do, and perhaps show to the band, when . . .

'KATRIONA!'

I was obviously in trouble.

I switched off Abandon Hope and hurried downstairs.

'Oops,' I said, when I saw the mess.

'While your dad's at the cash and carry aren't you supposed to be looking after these animals, Katriona McCrumble?' stormed Kirsty.

'Uh huh.'

'Then why is the floor covered in flour?'

Now I could have said, 'Because the malt whisky's in the flour jar, and if the flour had been in the flour jar . . .' etc., etc. – but I didn't. We McCrumbles can be known for our quick temper, and Kirsty's a lot older than me and has had much more practice, so instead I said, 'Max couldn't have liked the flour or he'd have eaten that up too.'

Kirsty reached for her mop. 'Get these creatures out of my kitchen and back to where they belong.'

'At once, or even sooner, Captain Kirsty,' I saluted, then had to dodge smartly as the wet mop threatened my ankles.

I called the dogs to heel. Millie, who'd been a silent witness throughout, came immediately. Max ignored me as usual, but Wilf came and stood by my side. Maisie's training perhaps. Max looked up. 'Gosh,' he thought. 'There goes my pal, Wilf. Perhaps I'd better go too. Wonder if he knows anywhere else that has food. Now that I've been really good and sick I'm a bit peckish again.'

So, to my surprise, I ended up with two collies and a wallaby by my side. I had been going to put Wilf back in his pen, but then I had a better idea.

'Walkies,' I said, and took the three of them along the shore road.

The tourists, wandering along admiring the scenery, were really surprised. One man was so busy looking at us he walked straight into the lamppost outside the post office, and another nearly ran his car off the road and into the loch. But the locals weren't surprised at all. They were used to seeing me out for a walk with a string of animals, usually dogs and donkeys, and the occasional cat, but a wallaby made a nice change.

'G'day, mate. How're you doin'?' said some, not realising Wilf had never been near Australia. If Wilf could have replied he'd probably have said, 'Aye, no sae bad, thanks,' in a broad Glaswegian accent.

'Wilf's fine,' I grinned. 'He's just raided Kirsty's larder, but he's still in one piece.'

Everyone stopped to chat and shake hands with the little wallaby with the black-tipped fingers. Wilf thoroughly enjoyed the attention. Max was delighted. He sat on the pavement wearing a pleased look. The one that said, 'Wilf is my pal. Isn't he great?'

Millie sat with a pleased look too. The one that said, 'Max is my son. Isn't he behaving well for a change? Not eating the tourists' crisps, or jogging their elbows so their ice creams land on the ground right beside him.'

We never really got a proper walk, just wandered along the shore road, chatting. When some of the tourists discovered Wilf lived at the inn, they decided to have dinner there, and followed us back to book a table.

Kirsty was delighted. 'That wallaby may be a menace in the kitchen,' she said, 'but he is good for business.' And she hurried along to James Ross, the butcher, for more supplies.

'Get out the blackboard,' she told me on her return, 'and write down Wallaby Wilf's recommendations for tonight.'

They were: Ozzie beef in beer, Ayres Rock chicken with paprika and Tasmanian apple tart, along with Kirsty's usual specialities.

That evening the inn was full. We had to turn people away. What's more, Wilf decided to sit with Millie and Max by the front door and greet the diners as they arrived. A kind of marsupial maitre d'. He was a big hit. A real star. He brought us business and everyone was happy. Perhaps with Wilf's help we'd be able to save up for our wildlife sanctuary quicker than we'd hoped.

We all thought everything was fine, except for Morag. As she helped me wait at tables that night she was a little bit quiet. Not her usual chatty self.

'What's the matter, Morag?' I asked. 'You're not

still worrying about Wilf? Look how well he's doing. He loves it here, and the Crumbling Arms has never been busier.'

But Morag just shook her head as she took a pile of empty pudding plates back into the kitchen.

'I feel what I feel, Kat,' she said quietly. 'I can't change that.'

To make matters even more perplexing, I saw Old Hamish that night. Tired out, after a busy night rushing about, I was trailing along to the bathroom in my old dressing-gown and slippers to clean my teeth, when I felt a sudden cold draught flowing up from the stairs. That could mean one of two things. Either the wind had got up and the front door had blown open or Old Hamish was around. It was a fine, still evening, so I stood perfectly still and waited.

Old Hamish's head appeared first as he floated up the stairs; his head with its long grey hair, and his face with its kindly expression. Then came his body in its old white shirt and McCrumble tartan plaid, caught over one shoulder by a large silver brooch. Finally came his McCrumble tartan kilt, worn and torn in places, followed by his legs encased in cross-gartered stockings.

Old Hamish floated over to me. I wasn't afraid of him. I had been, the first time I'd seen him, but now I knew he meant me no harm, quite the opposite, in fact. He usually appeared to me when trouble was brewing. He came to me as a kind of warning. Now he stood by me and put his hand on my arm. I felt no weight, only a slight chill. Then he looked at me kindly and disappeared.

I knew from past experience that the hand on my arm was a warning to be careful. But be careful of what? Or whom? First there was Morag with her 'feeling', and now there was Old Hamish with a ghostly hand on my arm.

'What does it all mean?' I thought rather crossly. 'What's going on? How am I supposed to understand it? Why can't the supernatural just get their act together and send me a text or an email!'

Chapter 13

Next day I wakened up with a really bright idea. I phoned Tina to say I'd be over to see her soon and hurried through my chores. First I had to help Dad in the kitchen. Martin Murray, our fishmonger, had just delivered some smoked haddock and I was cooking them for breakfast. Some people might think fish for breakfast is weird, but it's not. Kirsty taught me how to poach the fish in a little milk, then add some cream and a scattering of parsley at the finish. Yummy. The guest who had ordered it thought so too, and once other guests saw the haddock, they wanted the same.

Trouble is we usually serve poached haddock with

poached eggs, and I've never quite got the hang of cooking those. Kirsty's shown me a million times, but I still manage to make the poached eggs look like a one-eyed jellyfish with wispy tendrils. But I covered up the worst of the straggly bits with some triangles of toast and the guests didn't seem to mind. If anyone out there has a foolproof method for poaching eggs, please write, but don't send me an eggsample.

Breakfast over, I went out to feed the animals. Donk and Lily trotted over to get their carrots and have a chat. Wilf saw me and came over too. He munched on his oak leaves while I told them all about Abandon Hope. I would have brought down one of my posters to let them see, but they'd probably have eaten it. I told them how lucky they were to have their food served up to them by a charming waitress – what do you mean, who's that? – and that they didn't have to go searching on the estate, like the wildlife did. That's something Ron Jackson's always complaining about, how the wildlife take some of the game he thinks should just be for the estate guests to shoot. What does he want the wildlife to do, go to the local supermarket? I could just see the golden eagles going up and down the aisles with their trolley looking for something for supper.

'What do you fancy today, Pa? Couple of nice mice, perhaps.'

'Sounds good to me, Ma.'

'And we could wash them down with a tasty drop of spring water. How about that?'

'So long as it comes from a north-facing slope, Ma. You know I like my spring water well chilled.'

How ridiculous. And so is Ron Jackson. As I may have told him!

We still had our little eaglet staying with us. Kit Kat was doing well. After a few groggy days, he had perked up, and we would soon be able to take him out and release him back into the wild.

We had other animals staying with us too, while their owners were away. I topped up the peanuts in the cage of our three-legged hamster. His owners call him Hopalong, but he doesn't seem to mind. When I looked in, he was busy having a quiet snooze. He'd probably been up all night whizzing round on his wheel.

Lucy the rabbit was next, and I had some lettuce all ready. Some of that fancy rocket stuff Kirsty had spare. But Lucy ignored it, and immediately ate the bit of chocolate Kit Kat I offered.

Then I went to chat to Solly. He's a huge, overfed, fluffy grey moggy who only moves when he absolutely has to. His owner, old Mrs Corbet, carries him everywhere in her shopping basket. Solly hardly knows what his legs are for. I opened up his little house and placed his food just inside the door. From his comfortable bed at the far end, Solly gave me an incredulous, 'Do you really expect me to walk all the way over there to get that?' stare. 'Push the food closer, silly girl.'

'No chance, Solly,' I grinned at him. 'You want to eat, you come and get it.'

He still hadn't moved when I left. Probably hoping for a strong wind to blow the dish towards him, or for old Mrs Corbet to come hopping all the way over from the cottage hospital with her broken leg to coax him to eat. It was always a battle of wills between us whenever Solly came to stay. But I had always won. So far. He was pleased enough to board with us, though, because he likes Samantha. But she'll have nothing to do with him, snooty creature that she is. He has no pedigree, you see.

Finally there was Charlie, a cheerful little King Charles spaniel. He belongs to Mrs Lewthwaite who lives in the little white cottage beside the post office. She loves Charlie to bits. 'Much more than she's ever loved me,' her husband was known to complain in the bar of the Crumbling Arms, if anyone would listen.

Mrs Lewthwaite takes Charlie everywhere. Almost. The Lewthwaites go to visit Mr Lewthwaite's sister in Portugal for two weeks every year and leave Charlie with us. Mrs Lewthwaite doesn't want to leave Charlie. Mr Lewthwaite insists that she does. Charlie stays.

Mrs Lewthwaite always leaves me a list as long as a loo roll of Charlie's likes and dislikes, and she phones most days from Portugal to see if he's pining. Fat chance. Charlie always puts on a sad face till Mrs Lewthwaite leaves for her holiday, then he's ready to party. He and Millie and Max have a great time, and if they get into any trouble they always blame Charlie. He has such a sweet face, no one can ever be mad at him for long.

He gets away with everything. Like chewing a hole in the new leather slippers I had got Dad for his birthday. Dad wasn't pleased. Neither was I. The slippers had cost me a fortune, even if they were odd sizes – Dad has the same problem feet as me – and even if they were in the sale. But Charlie was unrepentant. I threatened to get Mrs Lewthwaite to stop his pocket money till the slippers were replaced, but he still didn't care. When his owner comes back he'll put on his sad little 'how could you go away and leave me like that?' face, and Mrs Lewthwaite will say she's sorry and spoil him rotten. Mrs Lewthwaite's an idiot and Charlie's a chancer.

Those are our boarders then, and when I'd attended to them, I set off for Tina's to tell her about my great idea. I told you about Tina's mum and dad and their little shop, didn't I? It doesn't make much money, so Mr and Mrs Morrison both give craft lessons in the village hall in wintertime, to help make ends meet. Mrs Morrison does spinning lessons and Mr Morrison teaches people how to throw pots, though the Nisbet boys were banned after they threw them at each other. I had been thinking about this when my great idea had come to me, and . . .

'Why don't you borrow Wilf for an afternoon?' I said to Tina, when I found her drooling over an Abandon Hope album cover in the empty shop.

'Borrow Wilf? Why?'

'Well, you saw how much custom he brought to the Crumbling Arms. So why don't you have Wilf along here? Might draw attention to the shop and bring in some business.'

'We could certainly do with it,' said Tina. 'Let's go and tell Mum and Dad.'

We found the Morrisons in one of the outbuildings at the back of the house. Mrs Morrison had her sleeves rolled up, and her hands were a fetching blue colour as she extracted dye from the leaves of some woad plants she'd grown. Mr Morrison was covered in red clay dust. Tina might complain that her parents were crazy, but they were also colourful.

And they were really enthusiastic about my idea.

'Good thinking, Kat,' they said. 'It's worth a try. Wilf could well attract some custom for us.'

And he did, but unfortunately not all of the right kind.

Chapter 14

I walked Wilf and the dogs along to Tina's that afternoon. I put a soft collar and a lead on Wilf and set off along the shore road. As usual, people stopped to talk. I told them all where we were going and invited them along to the Morrisons' shop. Unfortunately, on the way there, Wilf decided to visit another shop first. He saw someone come out of the post office with a handful of postcards and decided to investigate. He had hopped away from me and inside the post office before I could stop him. Now the post office is tiny. Two hitch-hikers with a map and it's full. Hardly room to swing a cat, never mind a wallaby with a mind of his own. And that mind had just decided it would be a good idea to investigate the revolving postcard rack Evie McCrumble was just restacking.

'Hullo, Wilf, come to buy a postcard?' she said, but that soon changed to 'Oh no, Wilf!' as he hopped round and round the rack with me in tow. Unfortunately the postcard rack wasn't as stable as the pine tree at Loch Lomond. Down it came, scattering the postcards everywhere.

'So sorry,' I said, as I tried to pick them up, unravel Wilf and stop him chewing a view of 'Sunset over Loch Bracken' at the same time.

Evie wasn't too pleased. She has arthritis in her fingers and it had taken her ages to stack that rack.

I offered to pay for the damaged postcards and got out of there as quickly as I could. I gave Wilf a severe talking-to. You know the kind of thing. 'Irresponsible behaviour. Should be more grown up at your age.' Threatened removal of Walkman, etc. He wasn't bothered at all, though he did behave the rest of the way along the road to Tina's. We went at a cracking pace. You wouldn't think hopping would be a fast way to travel, but Wilf could move, and I had to move with him. I arrived at Tina's puffed out.

'Practising for the Auchtertuie Highland Games, Kat?' she grinned, when she saw my red face.

I threw myself down on the grass just outside the shop and gathered my breath.

'I think I'll just stick to helping with the teas and coffees.'

Millie and Max lay down while Wilf looked around for more mischief. But I was keeping a close eye on him.

Tina looked beyond me to the gate at the bottom of their little front garden.

'You may be helping out with teas and coffees sooner than you think,' she grinned. 'You seem to have brought us some business already.'

'Not me,' I said. 'Wilf. I told everyone on the way along where we were going and some of them followed.

'Now, behave, Wilf,' I reminded him as a steady trickle of people came through the gate and stopped to admire him on their way into the shop. He behaved. Admiration he liked.

Mrs Morrison had organised free tea and coffee (but fortunately no home baking) for the customers, and they wandered round the shop, Mr Morrison's pottery mugs in hand, looking at the crafts. Many of them came out again clutching woollen purses, bags and belts and fantastically shaped pots. One man even had two bleached sheep's heads.

'Just what I needed for my garden,' he told Tina

and me. 'I'm making a desert garden with lots of spiky grasses and pebbles. The sheep's heads will help to give it that authentic wild west look; I haven't been able to find buffalo heads anywhere.'

It was only then that we noticed the cowboy hat hanging down his back and the spurs on his high-heeled boots.

That's when Ron Jackson appeared. He'd probably followed the line of people coming to the shop. He always liked to know what was going on in Auchtertuie, probably because no one liked him enough to tell him.

'Where did you get those sheep's heads?' he asked cowboy boots.

'Fantastic, aren't they? They're selling them in the shop. There are plenty more, though I think I got the prettiest.' And he wandered off happily, his spurs jingling.

Ron Jackson's eyes narrowed when he saw me and Wilf.

'That's a wild animal you've got roaming loose,' he said. 'It's dangerous. It should be locked up.'

'No, he shouldn't. He's not wild, he was born in captivity and is well used to people. Anyway,' I said, my temper rising, 'if anyone should be locked up it's you.'

Ron Jackson smiled nastily. 'Couldn't prove

anything though, could you? Even with your tame policeman.'

And he might have said more, but Millie had come over to my side. Brave Millie. She hates Ron Jackson, and usually keeps well out of his way, but she didn't like his tone or the way he was standing over me. Her ears went flat and her body tensed as she gave a low rumble in her throat. That alerted Max and Wilf. Max didn't know what was going on but started barking anyway. Wilf began hopping backwards and forwards in front of Ron Jackson. Perhaps he couldn't understand why this person wasn't admiring him. Ron Jackson looked at me as if to say something, then he looked at Wilf and the dogs and decided not to risk it. He turned and stomped off into the shop.

'Oh, Millie,' I said, dropping to my knees to cuddle her. 'Good girl. Brave girl.'

Millie relaxed; the tension dropped from her body and she stood there quivering. Max and Wilf looked at each other with an 'and what exactly was that all about?' expression.

'Whew,' said Tina. 'What a horrible man.'

And he hadn't finished. Probably because he'd come off worst in his encounter with the animals, Ron Jackson decided to make trouble in the shop. Tina and I heard raised voices and went to find out what was going on. Ron Jackson was now trying to bully Mrs Morrison.

'Where did those sheep's heads come from?' he demanded to know.

'From the sheep,' I muttered.

'You got them from the estate, didn't you?' he yelled at Tina's mum. 'You've been trespassing. That's an offence. So is stealing sheep's heads. I could have the law on you.'

'No, you couldn't,' I yelled back at him. 'You're just trying to cause trouble. There is no law of trespass in Scotland.'

'And the sheep's heads came from the Nisbets' hill farm,' said a bewildered Mrs Morrison. 'I've been nowhere near the estate.'

'So you can just take your false accusations and leave,' I said. 'And don't bother to come back.'

'Hear hear,' said the customers. 'What dreadful behaviour. You should be ashamed of yourself, a grown man like you.'

Ron Jackson glared at me. 'You haven't heard the last of me, Kat McCrumble,' he said. 'You or that stupid-looking wallaby.'

'He's not stupid,' I said, crossing my fingers behind my back. It was only a little lie. 'And he's a lot better looking than you'll ever be.'

Ron Jackson's face darkened.

'You'll be sorry you said that, miss,' he muttered, and left.

'Oh, well done, Kat,' said Tina. 'You showed him. I wish I was as brave as you and Millie.'

I gave her a half smile. 'I just get mad,' I said. 'And the anger fuels my tongue.' I knew I wasn't brave. I knew that inside I was quivering, just as Millie had been earlier. I also knew now that Morag and Old Hamish had been right. There was trouble ahead. Ron Jackson would make sure of it.

Chapter 15

Wilf's fame spread like warm syrup over pancakes, and soon a reporter/photographer, called Trevor, appeared from our local newspaper.

'There's always something happening around you, Kat McCrumble,' he said, pausing at the front door of the Crumbling Arms to pat Millie and Max. 'Last time I saw you you were catching badger baiters.'

'Not just me. I had some help,' I grinned. 'Most of Auchtertuie. It was a good night's work. Now I expect you want to see and hear all about our new "star".'

'Uh huh,' he nodded. 'He's making quite an impression hereabouts. Though I don't suppose you've heard any gossip about the possibility of even bigger stars coming to the hotel on the estate?'

'I never listen to gossip,' I said, crossing my fingers and my eyes. 'Why don't you come through to the back yard and I'll introduce you to Wilf.'

Wilf was having a rest under the shade of some chestnut trees at one side of his run, but he hopped over to say hullo when he saw us. Donk and Lily wandered over too.

'Hmm,' said Trevor, when he saw how well the animals got on. 'Perhaps I could get a shot of them all together. That would be unique. Might even make the nationals with a picture like that.' And he wandered round looking for the best angle for his photo shoot.

'Could you just pose them all for me, Kat?' he said.

'They're animals,' I said. 'Not supermodels. Just take them as they are.'

Finally Trevor decided the best shot would really be in front of the Crumbling Arms, so Donald dropped down from a nearby tree and led Donk and Lily while I took Millie, Max and Wilf round to the front of the inn.

'I'll try to get the name of the inn into the picture,' said Trevor. 'Little bit of publicity for you.'

I smiled and took Millie, Max and Wilf over to the front door to stand in front of Donk and Lily. It was a fine sunny day and the donkeys were wearing their old straw hats. I thought they looked really cute. So did they and kept nudging each other admiringly. Millie sat neatly and perfectly still in front of the camera. Wilf stood up straight and positively beamed. He was obviously used to having his photograph taken. Max wasn't. He turned round and showed his bum. Everyone laughed. It was typical Max behaviour. Trevor decided to try another shot with Max the right way round, but, before he could manage it, another animal strolled by and placed herself right in the centre of the group. Samantha. No one had seen where she'd come from, but as usual she'd been keeping an eye on things. Now, she really *was* a supermodel. You should have seen that cat preen.

Trevor took his pictures and went off quite happily, and the photo, along with the story of Wilf's arrival, appeared in our local paper the next day. Then it *was* picked up by the national papers. Wilf was news. Good news. People liked that and brought their children to see him. Some of them even wanted to stay at the inn. We didn't have enough room.

'What about the room you're keeping for that Australian Robert Swift,' I asked Dad. 'Couldn't you use that?'

'No,' said Dad. 'He has paid for it to be kept for

him till the end of the month and that's that.'

So all the overflow business went to the local bed and breakfast places. Everyone was delighted.

Well, nearly everyone. I was just managing to put Morag's feelings, Old Hamish's warnings and Ron Jackson's threats to the back of my mind when Morag brought us a letter.

Her face was anxious when she handed it over to Dad. 'It's not good news, Hector,' she said.

'It's the same kind of envelope as the ones we had before from C.P. Associates,' I said.

'Oh stop it, you two,' sighed Dad. 'It's just a plain white envelope. It's probably harmless. It's probably someone trying to sell us double-glazing or a new kitchen.'

But it wasn't.

'It's from C.P. Associates,' said Dad.

Morag and I made 'we told you so' faces.

He didn't notice.

'They want to buy Wilf,' he said.

'Whaaaat!' we chorused. 'Never!'

Dad read on. 'They say they can offer a better environment for him because they have much more land. That he would have more freedom. That it would be in his best interests.'

'Rubbish,' I cried. 'Since when did they become animal lovers? They just want him because he's bringing us business, and they want us closed down so they can turn this place into a tartan centre that will make them money.'

'Kat's right, Hector. What would they want with a little wallaby? Probably put him in a cage and exhibit him.'

I could feel my blood starting to boil. 'Tell them to back off, Dad,' I said. 'Tell them to take a running jump. Tell them to get lost. Tell them . . .'

'No?' suggested Dad.

'That too,' I said. 'But tell them forcibly, Dad. You're too nice.'

'Far too nice,' sighed Morag.

'I shall simply write and say that Wilf already has a good home and is certainly not for sale.'

'Good,' I said. 'Just think what Maisie would say.' Maisie had been phoning regularly to ask about Wilf, and I had been keeping her laughing with tales of his antics. 'She's going to visit us just as soon as she can get away. Things are a bit hectic for her just now with the zoo closing down.'

Morag nodded. 'I must get on now,' she said, and left to do the rest of her round.

Dad sat down to write to C.P. Associates. And all was quiet.

But not for long.

Chapter 16

A few days later we had an unexpected visit from the environmental health inspector. When he arrived I was in the kitchen, hovering round as Kirsty made her third batch of millionaire shortbread that morning. It's one of my favourites.

'Hullo, Roddy,' said Kirsty, up to her elbows in flour at the kitchen table. 'Nice to see you again. Pull out a chair and have some tea.'

'Er, not at the moment, thanks, Kirsty.' Roddy Chamber's face was embarrassed. 'This is an official visit.'

'An official visit?' frowned Kirsty. 'But didn't you inspect the inn only a couple of months ago?'

'Yes, but there's been a complaint.'

'From whom?' Kirsty picked up her rolling-pin.

Roddy looked startled, but she was only using it to roll out the shortbread.

'Can't say,' he said apologetically. 'But I have to follow it up and have a look around.'

'Look away,' said Kirsty, and carried on with her baking.

'I bet the complaint was from the big hotel,' I said. 'They're trying to put us out of business by using every trick they can.'

Roddy blew out his pink cheeks and headed for the stairs. 'I'll start at the top,' he muttered.

'The room with the PRIVATE KEEP OUT notice is mine,' I called, and wished I had made my bed.

After a while he appeared back in the kitchen. He looked in the pot Kirsty was stirring.

'Is that the caramel for the shortbread?' he asked.

'Uh huh,' said Kirsty. This uh huh simply meant yes.

'I have to inspect the kitchen now, Kirsty,' said Roddy.

'Uh huh.' This uh huh meant 'If you find the slightest speck of dirt in here, Roddy Chambers, you must have brought it in yourself!'

I grinned. I knew he wouldn't find anything wrong in the kitchen. *He* knew he wouldn't find anything wrong in the kitchen. He knew, like everyone else in Auchtertuie, that Kirsty was Little Ms Super Clean. Dirt was her enemy, and you don't want to be an enemy of Kirsty's, if you can help it. But Roddy Chambers did his job and inspected the kitchen anyway.

He pulled out the contents of cupboards, being very careful to replace them exactly as he'd found them. He examined his reflection in the gleaming pots hanging from their racks. He checked for any sign of mice – no sensible mouse would have dared. Animals were allowed in the kitchen only on Kirsty's say-so, and afterwards she double scrubbed everywhere they'd been. Roddy Chambers found nothing wrong.

'I shall report that the complaint is completely unfounded,' he said finally. 'Everything's in order, Kirsty.'

Kirsty gave him one of her looks.

'Not that I ever doubted it,' he added hastily. 'Now, did you mention something about tea?'

I grinned and pulled out a chair for him. Roddy Chambers had been in school with Kirsty. He knew she always got the Home Economics prize each year. He knew her nickname in school had been 'Squeaky' because she was so clean. He knew she would clean *him*, if he stayed still long enough.

'It was the big hotel that put in the complaint, wasn't it?' I said.

'I still can't say, Kat.'

'Right,' I said. 'Supposing I run through various names and you shake your head if they didn't make the complaint. That way you don't need to say anything. OK?'

'You are a very devious person, Kat McCrumble,' he smiled.

'Thank you,' I said. 'Now ... James Ross, the butcher.'

Roddy shook his head.

'Willie Ross, the policeman.'

Roddy shook his head.

'Someone from the big hotel.'

Roddy's head stayed still.

'Thank you,' I said. 'You didn't tell me anything. Well, not anything I didn't suspect.'

'They've got it in for us, right enough,' said Kirsty, spreading chocolate over the caramel on top of the shortbread. And she told Roddy about the dirty tricks that had been played in the past. 'You would think they would have more to do with their time,' she sniffed.

Roddy looked at his watch. 'Time I was off,' he said. 'As I said, I shall report back that the complaint was completely unfounded, and may, in fact, have been malicious. Who knows, the big hotel might be having an unexpected visit from an environmental health officer too, for wasting his valuable time.'

Kirsty smiled and gave him a tray of her millionaire shortbread to take away. 'Cut it in squares once the chocolate's properly set,' she said.

'Now this might look like a bribe, Kirsty McCrumble,' grinned Roddy.

'Not at all,' said Kirsty. 'It's not for you. It's for your mum.'

'That's all right, then,' said Roddy, and went off home to Fort William, where he lived with his mum.

Kirsty could do devious too.

When Dad came back from the cash and carry we told him what had happened.

'The big hotel are up to their tricks again,' he said, just as I had done.

I nodded. 'But they didn't get away with it. They may even be having an unexpected inspection of their own quite soon.'

And they did. Morag heard about it on her rounds.

'They weren't very pleased at the big hotel,' she said. 'Seems the inspection caused quite a bit of disruption and hotel guests were seriously inconvenienced.'

'Oh dear,' I said. 'That won't do the hotel's reputation any good. Serves them right, rotters that they are.'

But even I didn't realise just how rotten the rotters could be.

Three days later Wilf became ill. I discovered him lying on his side one morning when I went out to feed him.

'What's the matter, Wilf?' I cried, rushing up to him. 'What's wrong?' Wilf just looked at me mournfully and regurgitated a cud. It slid out of his mouth and on to the ground. Then he groaned and clutched at his middle.

I didn't know what was wrong with Wilf, but I knew he was in serious pain.

I raced back indoors. 'It's Wilf, Dad,' I gasped. 'He's really ill. Phone the vet.'

Fred Goldsmith, the vet from Fort William, came out as soon as he could.

Wilf was worse. His eyes were closed and his stomach was brick hard. Fred Goldsmith took one look and said, 'He's eaten something he shouldn't.' And he examined the cud that Wilf had brought up. 'It's fruit,' he sniffed. 'He's eaten too much fruit.'

'But we only give him the occasional banana,' I

said. 'As a treat. We know too much fruit upsets him.'

Fred Goldsmith felt Wilf's stomach. 'There's a lot more than one banana in there. There's a lot of gas in there. I'll have to put down a tube to pump his stomach. That'll relieve his pain.'

I watched closely. The vet gave Wilf a little injection to sedate him then passed a tube gently down Wilf's throat. Soon the contents of Wilf's stomach were in the bottom of a bucket.

Fred Goldsmith examined them. 'As I thought,' he said. 'Fruit.'

'Poor little Wilf,' I said, stroking his head as he came round from his anaesthetic. 'What a terrible time you've had. But where did you get all the fruit? I wish you could tell me.'

'Probably got into the kitchen somehow,' said Dad, 'and pinched all the apples for Kirsty's tarts.'

But he hadn't.

'I keep all the fruit in the big fridge in the pantry just now, Kat,' said Kirsty, 'to prevent it getting overripe in this warm weather. There's no way Wilf could get in there for I have the door locked.' And she went into her apron pocket and brought out the key. 'Wilf must have got the fruit from somewhere else.'

'But he was fine last night when I settled him

down,' I said. 'He must have eaten the fruit during the night.'

'Or someone's given it to him,' frowned Kirsty. 'But everyone round here knows not to feed him fruit, so who would do a thing like that?'

There was only one person I could think of, and there are no prizes for guessing who that might be.

Chapter 17

It's about now that Kirsty and I have our one really big row of the year. It's the annual buying-of-the-school-uniform battle. It's not quite as bad as the famous battles of Flodden and Culloden, but nearly. Basically Kirsty insists that we go to Inverness to replace the previous year's school uniform, because it now looks so bad that even the scarecrows would refuse to wear it. And basically I disagree because . . .

1. I don't like school uniforms. I especially don't like wearing a new school uniform which always feels stiff and uncomfortable to me. And I have to wear it at the hottest time of the year. Why is

it that the best weather always appears the first day back in school after the summer holidays? Sun streams in the classroom windows and I sit there, sweltering, in a new school blazer which looks as though it's been bought for a much taller, much curvier female, with arms like a gorilla and bosoms like a shelf. My last blazer was so big I could have camped in it. OK, I admit I did grow a bit in the year but still . . .

2. I don't see why pupils should have to wear school uniform anyway. Teachers don't. They can swan around in whatever they like. Like our English teacher, Miss Erikson. She's of Viking origin, she says, though I've never seen her wear the helmet. But, in hot weather, she wears a long, flowing, pink crinkle-cotton skirt and pink T-shirt. She's pale and blonde and cool and comfortable, while I sit there looking like a beetroot with a suntan. Of course, I mentioned this to her. Went on a bit about it, actually. Asked her if we couldn't just wear our normal clothes. Asked her if she thought it was fair that we got so hot and sticky. Said I thought we might work better in jeans and a T-shirt . . . She said I talked too much. That a school rule was a school rule. But you know what they say about rules, don't you . . .

3. I'd rather spend the money on something else. Like new jeans and a T-shirt. But Kirsty insists that we buy the uniform. I know she's just trying to look after me because I've no mum. I know she just wants me to go to school looking semi-respectable, but we have the battle anyway.

The trip to Inverness was arranged for the end of the week. I did everything I could to get out of it. Said I had to look after the animals. Donald volunteered to do it. Said we were too busy and who would help with the lunches. Morag volunteered to do it. Said I was sure I was coming down with flu, chickenpox, the Black Death, etc. No one was convinced; I had to go.

We set off early in Kirsty's old mini. It's white with a black roof and a mind of its own. It also has a name of its own. It's called Shona. Don't ask me why. Kirsty talked to Shona as we drove along. 'Now, we're coming to a bit of a hill here, Shona,' she said. 'But we'll take it in third gear and you'll be fine . . . There now, that wasn't so bad, was it? Now, just watch out for this lorry. When he slows down, get ready to scoot past him. OK?'

I wouldn't have been at all surprised if Shona had replied. But I was quiet. I was doing my huffy bit. And I was lasting well till I spotted a whole field of lapwings and shouted, 'Look, Kirsty. Look, Shona. Peewees.' Now I was talking to the mini too. Crazy or what?

We arrived in Inverness in time for lunch and went to a little café Kirsty knows. The food was good, though not as good as Kirsty's. Then it was time for the dreaded uniform buying. We left the café and headed down a side street to an old-fashioned shop with LADIES' AND GENTS' OUTFITTERS written in faded gold lettering above the door. An elderly shop assistant, who smelled faintly of tea roses, remembered us.

'Oh, it's you again,' she said faintly, in a voice that suggested she had only just recovered from last year's visit. Then she remembered her manners and added, 'How nice to see you.' But I don't think she meant it. It's not that I'm difficult to fit. It's just that I stand there in silent protest (can you believe silent?), stiff as a tailor's dummy, resentment coming from every pore, while Kirsty and the shop assistant try things on me and discuss how I look. Some people don't like going to the dentist's, but I think buying the school uniform is much worse. Eventually, after much poking and tweaking, I had a new giant-sized blazer I would be able to carry Wilf inside, a school skirt and trousers that would fit if I developed beanstalk tendencies, and several school shirts with enough room at the neck for your average bulldog. And I was getting seriously fed up being told to stand up straight. Kirsty thought about attempting to buy me a new school sweater too, but read the warning signs – I do a really good line in loud tutting and sighing – and we headed for home, stopping only for Kirsty to visit the wool shop.

We listened to some Abandon Hope tapes on the way back, so the journey was quite pleasant, till Shona decided to overheat and we had to stop and give her some of the spring water Kirsty kept in the car.

'She much prefers it to tap water,' she said. I didn't ask her how she knew.

Despite Shona's eccentricities, Kirsty and I arrived back at the Crumbling Arms in one piece, and were almost back speaking to each other.

'And we're just in time to prepare the evening meals too,' said Kirsty, and gave Shona a 'well done' pat.

I carried my parcels into the hall just as Dad appeared from the kitchen. He looked worried. 'What's the matter?' I said. 'What's happened? Is Wilf sick again?'

'Wilf's disappeared,' he said.

I dropped the parcels. 'How? Where? I thought Donald was looking after him.'

'He was. Donald was in the back yard attending to the boarders, and when he looked round, Wilf had gone. Millie and Max picked up his scent. He was headed into the estate. Donald's there with the dogs now, looking for him.'

'I knew I shouldn't have gone for that stupid school uniform,' I said, and kicked the parcels.

'Don't worry,' said Dad. 'If anyone can find him, Donald can.'

But he didn't. Donald and Millie and Max didn't come back until the light had failed. But there was no Wilf.

Donald was anxious. 'Millie and Max were on his trail for a while and I was sure we would find him at any moment. But then, all of a sudden, the trail went cold. The dogs circled round and round, but nothing. Wilf seemed to have completely disappeared.'

'Millar's pond,' I said, suddenly frightened. It's a horrible stagnant pond some way into the estate.

Donald shook his head. 'The trail led in the other direction. I'll go out looking again at first light. I'm really sorry, Kat.'

I gave him a hug. 'He could just as easily have

disappeared while I was around,' I said. 'We're sure to find him tomorrow.'

But we didn't. We searched and searched, but there was no sign of Wilf. Word soon spread that he was missing, and people searched their garden sheds and outhouses to see if he'd been accidentally shut in somewhere, but nothing. Morag kept a lookout on her rounds too, as did Martin Murray in his fish van, but Wilf seemed to have vanished into thin air.

Chapter 18

Wilf was missing for three days. I was sick with worry. Each morning Donald and I went into the estate. We didn't care if Ron Jackson spotted us or not, we had to find Wilf. Donald took Max and headed off through the trees towards Ben Bracken. I took Millie and stayed closer to the lochside. I checked around Flip's sett. Flip was used to meeting animals in the Crumbling Arms, and had encountered Wilf in the kitchen one night, not long after Wilf had arrived. As usual Flip had poked his nose through the cat flap and had a sniff. Hmm, something smelled different. Obviously Wilf. 'It's all right, Flip,' I'd told him. 'Wilf's a pal, and he doesn't eat cat food.' Reassured, Flip had squeezed the rest of himself through the cat flap and headed for Samantha's dish. He didn't let much get in the way of his dinner. Certainly not a cheeky wee wallaby.

So, it was just possible Wilf could have met up with Flip. But there was no sign of any wallaby tracks at the sett. Nothing that seemed unusual. I knew that in the wild, wallabies often rested up during the day, so perhaps Wilf was concealed somewhere. I called his name. Over and over. But there was still no sign of him. Millie had her nose constantly to the ground, but could catch no scent either. We glimpsed the occasional deer, bounding off as we approached. Rabbits and mice scurried away from us into the undergrowth, and buzzards watched us as they wheeled overhead in the thermal currents. I just wished they could have told us where Wilf was.

I was worried about him surviving on his own. I knew food wasn't a problem, there was plenty of that about. He could even live on heather if he had to, but Wilf was used to being looked after, and not very forest wise. And supposing he had fallen and broken a leg or hopped into a metal trap. They were supposed to be illegal, but knowing how Ron Jackson felt about the wildlife, I couldn't be sure there were none. But I found nothing.

Miserably, I trailed back home with Millie each night. On the third evening of Wilf's disappearance, the inn seemed extra full, and Kirsty, Morag and Dad were rushed off their feet trying to cope. I had just washed my hands and tidied myself, and was crossing the hall behind Dad to help in the dining room, when the front door burst open and two visitors came in. One was very welcome, one was not. It was Wilf . . . with Ron Jackson.

'Wilf,' I cried, and flew to his side. 'Are you all right?'

Wilf reached for my hair.

'*He's* all right, but my new seedlings aren't,' snarled Ron Jackson. 'Just look at this.' And he thrust a handful of trampled seedlings at Dad. 'How am I supposed to get on with the reforestation of the estate if you let wild animals like this roam free? He's undone years of work. I'm reporting this to the authorities. You people are obviously not fit to look after animals.' And he removed the rope he had around Wilf's neck and left.

Dad and I were too taken aback to reply. 'I'll see to Wilf,' I said, and quickly got him out of the hall and into his pen in the back yard. 'Where have you been?' I asked him. 'What happened to you? Oh, I wish you could tell me.'

But he couldn't. He looked a little bewildered, but otherwise unharmed.

I was still making a fuss of him when Donald and Max returned.

'Oh, thank goodness he's back,' said Donald. 'Where did you find him?'

'I didn't,' I said grimly. 'Ron Jackson did.' And I told him what had happened.

Donald frowned. 'I passed the reforestation part of the estate earlier,' he said, 'and the seedlings were fine. No sign of any wallaby tracks around there and Max got no scent at all.'

'This is probably just another attempt to put us out of business, then,' I said. 'We won't let the estate have Wilf so they're trying other methods to get rid of him.'

'Wilf's so friendly,' said Donald. 'He would go with anyone who would feed him. Who knows where he's been these last few days? Certainly not on the estate or we'd have found him. I wouldn't be surprised if Ron Jackson had him locked up somewhere. I bet he uprooted the seedlings himself.'

'We'll probably never know,' I muttered. 'And we'll certainly never be able to prove anything. We know how good he is at covering his tracks.'

Donald and I took Wilf out to his pen and left

Millie guarding him. When we went back inside Dad met us, grim faced. 'I've just had Constable Ross on the phone,' he said. 'Ron Jackson's already made his complaint, and has said that if he catches Wilf on the estate again, he'll shoot him.'

We had to lock Wilf in one of the outhouses that night. We didn't want to, but we couldn't risk him wandering off.

'Sorry, Wilf,' I said, when I'd made him as comfortable as I could. 'But it's the best we can do at the moment.'

'I'll keep a lookout during the night,' said Donald, and headed for the nearest oak tree.

Dad and I went back into the inn and saw to the evening guests as best we could. Sometimes it's hard to put on a smiley face when you're really worried inside. Finally the last of the guests left. Dad and I were just closing up when a hire car drew up outside the inn. A grizzled man unfolded his long, lean body from the driver's seat and strode to the front door.

'Ah,' he said, 'glad I caught you before you locked up. Sorry I'm so late.' And he thrust out a large, leathery hand to Dad. 'I believe you've kept a room for me. I'm Rob McCrumble Swift from the Gold Coast in Australia.'

Chapter 19

We discovered that Rob McCrumble Swift was the easiest guy in the world to get along with, and we sat in the kitchen talking late into the night. Kirsty and Morag were long gone, so I buttered some of Kirsty's bannocks and made a pot of tea for us all. Dad and I told Rob all about the Wilf problem. It was pressing on our minds and seemed the natural thing to do.

'I expect you know all about kangaroos and wallabies,' I said, 'coming from Australia.'

'I know a bit,' smiled Rob. 'I rescue some of the little ones.'

'You have a wildlife sanctuary too,' I gasped.

'Kind of. Y'see, the 'roos are none too clever and have no road sense at all . . .'

'A bit like our hedgehogs and pheasants,' I muttered.

'. . . and a lot of them get knocked down by cars. If a mother is killed, her joey is left to fend for himself, so I try to look after the orphans as best I can. I design golf courses for a living, so when I'm asked to design a course, I make it a condition that there should be a bit of land left aside for orphaned joeys. I build feeding troughs on it for them so that they don't go hungry. I don't need to worry about water troughs. 'Roos and wallabies can go without water for months and are good at finding their own. Dig little water wells, in fact. I own a small golf course, and it's a fine sight at sundown to see all the animals hopping down to the trough to eat.'

I knew I liked this fellow.

But that still didn't solve the problem of Wilf.

'It's a tricky one,' said Rob, running a hand through his wiry hair. I wondered idly if mine would be like that when I was his age. If so, Kirsty would probably turn me upside down and use me as a pot scourer. A good use for you at last, Kat McCrumble, she'd say.

'You may have to face the fact,' went on Rob, 'that the Crumbling Arms may not be the best home for Wilf, after all . . .'

'Oh, but it is,' I protested. 'The zoo is closing

down and Maisie wanted him to go to a good home and we love him . . .'

'Sometimes that's not enough, Kat,' said Dad gently. 'We have to consider what's best for Wilf. We can't keep him locked up for ever, and we can't risk having him fed too much fruit again, or worse still, shot.'

'But he didn't touch those seedlings,' I cried. 'I'm sure he didn't. It makes me so angry to think that he's getting the blame for something he didn't do. It's not fair.'

Dad patted my hand. 'Kat hates unfairness,' he told Rob. 'Gets quite fierce about it sometimes.'

'Quite right too,' said Rob. 'But there is one solution . . . I could take him home with me, if you like.'

There was a small silence.

'Take him to Australia?' I said, as though Australia was on the other side of the moon.

'It's not such a bad place,' grinned Rob. 'We have electricity and hot and cold running water now. Here, have a look at these photos and you'll see.' And he went into his wallet and produced a handful of snaps.

'See, this is where I live, near Surfer's Paradise, on the Gold Coast.'

His house overlooked the sea. It was a long low

building with a veranda running all the way round. The garden was lush with greenery and bright with grey and pink galahs flying through the trees. 'Look at the beaches and giant surf,' I said to Dad. 'And the windsurfers in their skimpy shorts.' We get windsurfers on Loch Bracken sometimes, but they always wear winter wet suits, even in the summertime. Especially in the summertime.

'And here's my little golf course.'

It didn't look very little to me, and it had trees planted all over it to give the golfers shade from the fierce summer sun.

'Look at those enormous poinsettia bushes,' I exclaimed. 'We only ever get tiny poinsettia pot plants at Christmas time, and they've usually always lost all their red bracts by the New Year. Oh, and look at the kangaroos and wallabies.'

'That's them hopping in for their tucker,' said Rob. 'Sometimes wallabies can be quite solitary creatures, but if Wilf's been raised in a zoo, he'll be used to company.'

Dad said nothing, just waited for me to come to my own conclusion.

I turned the problem round and round in my head. I could only see one way out.

'We'd have to talk to Maisie,' I said at last. 'We couldn't do anything with Wilf without her permission. And I just hate the thought that C.P. Associates and Ron Jackson have won and that we'll lose Wilf . . .'

'Ah, C.P. Associates,' said Rob. 'I was going to talk to you about them. How much do you know about them?'

'Not much,' said Dad.

'Except that they're rotten and horrible and want to put us out of business. And they give orders to Ron Jackson to harass us whenever he can. And I'd like to meet them face to face and tell them exactly what I think of them.' I paused for breath.

'Kat doesn't care much for them,' smiled Dad.

'Me neither,' Rob smiled at me. 'But they're partly why I'm here.'

'Oh?'

'They're thinking about adding a golf course to the estate and have asked me to design it for them.'

Dad frowned. 'But where would they put it? The only flat land around here is in our back yard and in the forest beyond it.'

'That's right,' said Rob. 'I've studied various maps.'

'But what about the wildlife?' I cried. 'What about the badgers? What about Flip? He's our semi-tame badger,' I explained to Rob. 'What about the red squirrels and the deer and the birds . . .'

'C.P. Associates don't much care.'

I sat back. Stunned.

'The reason it's taken me so long to get here,' Rob explained, 'is that I was doing some checking up on C.P. Associates. I always like to know who I'm working for and what they're like. I was intrigued when they wrote to me about this project, especially as it was in McCrumble country, and, as I'd always promised myself a visit here one day, I thought I might combine the two.'

'And now you're going to design a golf course for them . . .' My face was stony.

'No, Kat,' Rob said quietly. 'I'm not, but I have to try to make sure no one else does either, so I've been preparing a report, listing all the difficulties in the project, in an effort to put them off.'

'But will they believe you?' I said. 'You're a McCrumble.'

'They don't know that. They don't know McCrumble is my middle name. And there's something else.'

What next, I thought. I felt as though my brain was in meltdown.

'I found out what C.P. stands for. It's Castor and Pollux.'

'The heavenly twins,' I gasped. 'Sons of Zeus in Greek mythology.'

See, I do listen in school sometimes.

Rob nodded. 'But the company's not owned by two men. Only one.'

'Who's that?' asked Dad and I.

Rob paused. 'His name's Callum McCrumble.'

'Callum McCrumble!' I could hardly take it in. 'You mean it's a McCrumble who's trying to put us out of business and who's been doing all these rotten things?'

'Looks like it,' said Rob.

'Then it's just like the legend,' I said. 'Old Hamish's twin brother was called Callum and he was a rotter too.'

'I've heard the legend,' said Rob.

'Well, that's certainly given us something else to think about,' said Dad. 'But in the meantime our most pressing problem is still what to do about Wilf.'

I dragged my mind back. 'I know we have to do what's best for him,' I admitted. 'Even if it does mean losing him . . . I'll phone Maisie in the morning . . .'

'That's a very grown-up decision, Kat,' said Dad, and Rob nodded in agreement.

Grown-up? I didn't want to be grown-up. I wanted to get hold of Callum McCrumble and shake him till his teeth rattled. I wanted to sneak up behind

Ron Jackson and boot him on his beefy backside. I wanted to keep Wilf with us. But that didn't look like being possible now. Oh . . . it was all getting to be too much. I gave a deep sigh and stood up to go to bed. Suddenly I was very tired. Suddenly I didn't want to have to make decisions. Suddenly I had the feeling that being grown-up wasn't all it was cracked up to be.

Chapter 20

I phoned Maisie next morning after breakfast. Donald had let Wilf out, and he was in the back yard playing with Millie and Max and Charlie, the King Charles spaniel. They were playing their favourite game of chasing round Wilf, who was in the middle of them, quite happy. But I knew Ron Jackson and Callum McCrumble had it in for Wilf, and I knew we couldn't be with him twenty-four hours a day. Even Donald couldn't keep watch from his tree all the time.

Maisie answered the phone and listened very quietly while I told her what had happened.

Then she said, 'I can see the problem's getting worse, Kat. And we certainly must do what's best for Wilf. I know he can be tricky at times, and that makes it so easy for people to blame him for anything that happens.'

Then she spoke to Dad and to Rob. He promised to send her details of his animal rescue work in Australia. That way she would know what sort of a place Wilf would be going to, if she decided to send him there. Maisie said she would think about it and that she would be up to see Wilf soon. Hopefully in time for the Auchtertuie Highland Games. Then she rang off, a bit upset.

I was pretty glum too and only cheered up when Dad said, 'I'll keep an eye on Wilf; why don't you and Donald take Kit Kat out and set him free? He's perfectly all right now, and we don't need to keep him any longer.'

'OK,' I said, and immediately felt a little better. Dad knew I just loved being able to return animals and birds back to the wild.

Donald and I put Kit Kat in a cage. We placed him carefully in the back of our old van and drove to the foot of Ben Bracken. The road runs past the field where the Highland Games are held, then peters out on to a gravel track. We got Kit Kat out of the van and began to head up the Ben. Kit Kat immediately started to dance excitedly from one claw to the other.

'Do you think he senses he's going home?' I asked Donald.

'Who knows?' smiled Donald. 'But if I were a golden eagle, I'd be happy living in a place like this.'

We climbed the difficult, heavily wooded slope till we came to an area where we thought there would be a good updraught to help Kit Kat on his way. We put the cage down on a reasonably level piece of ground, opened the door and stood well back, behind some trees. Kit Kat looked out of the cage, then hopped out. He seemed to take a moment to gather himself, then he spread his wings and took off up into the treetops. He sat there for a little then opened his wings and took off again, soaring upwards till he was floating in and out of the clouds. We watched as he wheeled round and round, testing his wings.

'Can you imagine how that must feel?' said Donald. 'To be free like that after being locked up.'

'I think I can,' I said. 'And perhaps Wilf will feel like that too if we let him go to Australia to be with the other wallabies.'

Donald patted my arm. He knew I wanted to do the best for Wilf, but he knew I was hurting just the same.

When we got home, I phoned Tina to tell her

what had happened. She was pleased about Kit Kat and very sympathetic about Wilf.

'Poor little Wilf,' she said. 'But I know you'll do what's right, Kat.'

After that I went out into the yard to feed Donk and Lily and to keep an eye on Wilf. I was just chatting to the donkeys when Morag arrived in her post office van. She always drives into the back yard so that she can give the dogs their treats, then she comes into the kitchen for her cup of tea.

Morag looked at my glum face. She didn't need the second sight to know that there was something wrong. She sat at the kitchen table while I relayed the events of the night before. She was enraged about C.P. Associates turning out to be a McCrumble.

'Must be descended from the original Callum,' she decided. 'Not from Old Hamish like us.' But she didn't say, 'I told you so', when I told her about Wilf. Instead she said quietly, 'I think you made the right decision, Kat. I know you feel bad about losing Wilf, but just think how much worse it would be if Ron Jackson got him in his sights.'

I knew she was right.

Morag gave me a hug and Kirsty gave me another scone. 'Every cloud has a silver lining,' she said. 'If

Wilf goes to Australia, perhaps one day you can go out to visit him.'

'Perhaps,' I said, still not happy.

'Or perhaps I have news that might cheer you up,' said Morag.

'You haven't "seen" Ron Jackson fall headfirst into a barrel of treacle after being chased by the Loch Bracken sea monster, have you?'

Morag shook her head.

'Pity.'

'But I *have* spoken to Henry McCrumble's wife, Lottie's, second cousin, Sarah.'

'And?'

'Abandon Hope are at the big hotel. They arrived last night. Sarah served them breakfast this morning.'

'No!'

'Yes! Do you want to know what they had to eat?'

'Yes! No! Tell me later. I must phone Tina again. Right away.'

Tina came over right away, her eyes shining. 'Is it true, Kat? Are they really here?' she asked, when I met her outside the inn. I was picking up the litter stupid people had dropped. Litter makes me mad. I know a lot of things make me mad, and litter is one of them. Whether it's broken glass left by the lochside for children and dogs to cut themselves on, or lead weights abandoned by fishermen that the swans choke on, or greasy chip boxes that get blown into our holly bushes by the front door, it makes me angry. I put the greasy chip boxes in the nearby bin, wiped my hands on my jeans and hugged Tina.

'It's true,' I said. 'Morag told me a little while ago.'

'Morag?' Tina's face fell. 'Did she "see" them in one of her trances or does she really know?'

'She really knows. They arrived at the big hotel yesterday.'

'Wow!' said Tina. 'If they're really here, they could appear at any minute.' And she looked along the street. But the street only held the usual people going about their normal business. There was Jinty McCrumble out with her squeezy mop, washing the bakery_window. There was James Ross, the butcher, rolling out his blue and white striped canopy against the morning sun. There was Henry McCrumble putting up his posters advertising the Auchtertuie Highland Games. But there was no utterly delicious, totally delectable, scrummily scrumptious boy band.

Henry McCrumble saw us and came over. He handed me a couple of posters.

'Would you put these up in the inn, Kat?' he said.

'We want to get a good crowd at the Games.'

'Do you know what the weather's going to be like yet?' I grinned.

'No,' he said. 'I'll speak to Morag nearer the time, or failing that, watch the weather forecast on the TV. Och, but they don't always get it right. Said it would be fine last year and we had a downpour. I should have listened to Morag.'

I nodded. 'I was helping in the tea tent and we were run off our feet when everyone rushed in at the same time.'

'Aye, and big Andy McClumpha slid on the wet grass and dropped his caber on his big toe,' sighed Henry. 'He's judging the Bonnie Baby competition this year instead.' Then he looked round and lowered his voice. 'Do you happen to know if Kirsty's intending to enter the piping competition this year again?'

'I don't know. But she might be. She's very keen.'

'Aye, right enough,' muttered Henry. 'I must remember to put my earplugs into my sporran, just in case.' And he wandered off with the rest of his posters.

Tina grinned at me. 'Will you be entering for the Highland dancing competition, Kat?'

'Nope. I gave that up when I was six. I came ninth, out of eight entrants. The only dancing I'll be doing will be to Abandon Hope. Now I have a plan to try to get to see them.'

'You always have a plan.'

'It's not much of a one,' I admitted. 'It mainly involves sneaking into the forest, sneaking on to the estate and sneaking up to the hotel grounds.'

'That's a lot of sneaking.'

'Thank you. It's what I do best.'

'Should we be risking it, though?' worried Tina. 'After what Ron Jackson said about Wilf? He might be looking out for him and catch us instead.'

'He might. But Ron Jackson's a bully and you either stand up to bullies or they walk all over you.'

'You're so fierce, Kat.'

'No, I'm not,' I grinned. 'I've just seen the size of Ron Jackson's feet.'

So we agreed to go. I checked first with Dad on the whereabouts of Wilf. He was fine. Dad and Donald were trying to make Wilf's pen more secure, and Wilf and Millie and Max were 'helping'. They'd be there all day. Knowing that Wilf was safe, Tina and I slipped off across our back yard and into the forest.

A few metres in, the forest gets really thick, and we were soon deep in the gloomiest part.

'I'm glad I'm with you, Kat,' shivered Tina. 'I wouldn't like to be here on my own. It's a bit scary.'

'Not when you get to know it,' I said. I had been roaming the forest since I was little. Donald, who knew every tree, had taught me many landmarks and secret pathways. The forest was my friend.

We pressed on through the trees, pausing every now and then to listen to the tap-tapping of a woodpecker, or to catch a glimpse of a siskin or a tree pipit. Rabbits scattered before us, and whirring from the treetops said the wood pigeons were about. But everything kept out of our way. We were the interlopers. The forest was their home.

The forest floor grew dank and fallen trees hindered our progress as we drew near Millar's pond. It was eerily still and covered in grey-green algae. No one knew how deep it was. As always there was a dead feel around it. No birdsong here.

Tina shivered. 'I don't like this bit of the forest. It gives me the creeps.'

'Me too,' I admitted, 'but we'll be past it in a few moments.'

That's when we heard some unusual noises. The sound of dry twigs snapping. The sound of harsh voices and muttered cursing.

'Quick,' I whispered to Tina. 'Hide behind that big oak. That could be Ron Jackson, and if he spots us we're in trouble.'

'I suppose it could just be Abandon Hope out for a walk,' said Tina.

I shook my head. 'It doesn't feel like Abandon Hope. I think I would know if Micky was around.'

Help! Now I was getting to be as bad as Morag.

We stood still, hardly daring to breathe, as the voices came nearer. They were men's voices, rough and gravelly. But there was another noise too, a kind of snuffling and whining. A dog? I frowned. Surely it couldn't be the badger baiters and their dogs. We'd had trouble with them before, but this was the wrong time of day. They usually got up to their evil deeds at night-time. The voices stopped but the snuffling and whining continued, followed by a terrified bark. What was going on? I could stand it no longer. My McCrumble nose got the better of my common sense and I stuck my head round the side of the tree to have a look.

Two men stood by the edge of Millar's pond. They were half turned from me, but seemed to be tying something up in a heavy black bin sack. The snuffling and whining grew louder, followed by more terrified barking and yelping. Then, before my eyes, the men lifted up the sack and . . .

'Stop! What are you doing! Stop!' I yelled. I broke cover and ran full pelt towards them. But they didn't stop. They hurled the sack into the pond and turned towards me.

'Och, it's only a daft wee lassie,' they laughed. 'Ignore her. What can she do?' And they made off, crashing through the trees.

I ran to the edge of Millar's pond, Tina at my heels.

'What is it, Kat?' she panted. 'What did you see?'

'They threw a poor dog in there to drown,' I said. 'I'm going in after it.'

'Kat, you can't.' Tina was aghast. 'It's a horrible pond. You don't know what's down there.'

'There's a poor defenceless dog down there, Tina,' I said. 'There's no time to lose.' And I kicked off my trainers and jumped in, feet first.

Now I know I jump into a lot of things feet first, without thinking, but I wasn't that stupid. I had seen where the dog went in and had noted the ripples on the pond. I swam towards the spot. Grey-green algae clung to me and the water felt oily. I trod water where I thought the dog had gone in, took a deep breath and dived down. Yuk. It was murky down there. I couldn't see a thing. The algae cut off most of the light from the surface. I swam around in what I thought was a circle till my breath gave out. Then I surfaced with a gasp, feeling the algae coating my hair and my face.

'Kat, thank goodness. Oh, Kat, come out. Please come out,' yelled Tina.

But I plunged back down again, the sound of that terrified bark still in my ears. I swam around once more. The dog had to be here somewhere and I didn't have much time. I kicked out and my foot caught on something. I turned round and felt for it. I couldn't believe it, it was a supermarket trolley. The litter louts had been here too. I was about to thrust it away from me when I realised there was something in it. I reached in. It felt like a plastic sack. I grabbed it and hauled it to the surface. It was the right sack, I was sure of it. As fast as I could I towed it to the edge of the pond and hauled it out.

'Grab the sack and open it quick,' I yelled to Tina.

We tore at it with our fingers. The heavy-duty plastic stretched under our efforts but wouldn't give way.

'A stick,' I yelled. 'We need a stick.'

I flew to the nearest tree, pulled off a small lower branch and pierced the plastic with the jagged edge. Then I stuck my finger in and pulled. A small hole appeared and we both got a finger in it and pulled as hard as we could. The plastic gave way. A long thin dog, his ribs showing clearly against his pale skin, lay inside the sack. His eyes were closed. He was hardly breathing. I didn't really know what to do, but I gently opened his mouth and started breathing into it. For a moment I thought I was too late, but then his eyes opened and he coughed and shuddered and took in great gulps of air.

'Oh thank goodness,' I gasped.

'He's a greyhound,' said Tina, peeling the rest of the sack away from him. 'A beautiful greyhound, and not very old. Why would anyone want to drown such a lovely dog?'

'I don't know,' I said grimly, trying to soothe the frightened animal as best I could. 'But I'm going to find out.'

Chapter 21

To say Dad was upset at me jumping into Millar's pond is putting it mildly. He was apoplectic, white faced, starey eyed, almost stuttering with anger and anxiety.

I suppose I must have looked a bit of a sight, staggering back to the Crumbling Arms, sopping wet, covered in algae, carrying a greyhound.

Dad was wet too, but only as far as his upper arm where he'd been clearing a drain blocked by Max's rubber ball. Millie, who'd been watching the drain unblocking with interest, spotted me first and barked a greeting as she bounded over. Dad and Donald looked up and immediately hurried over to take charge of the greyhound.

'You're soaked through, Kat,' said Dad, as he ushered us all into the kitchen. 'How did you get into such a mess? What on earth happened?'

'Some men threw the dog into Millar's pond,' I panted. 'I had to get him out before he drowned.'

Dad paused in his examination of the dog.

'You went into Millar's pond?' He was incredulous.

I nodded, suddenly feeling a little bit wobbly.

'It was the only way I . . . there was no time to . . . the dog was in a sack . . . there were two horrible men . . .' I paused, as I saw the really angry look on Dad's face. 'Good thing I got my swimming certificate in Brownies,' I added, as though that would help.

Of course it didn't.

'You took on two criminals. You jumped into that vile water, infested with heaven knows what, to look for a sack!' Dad's tone was icy. 'And just what, exactly, were you using for brains at the time, Katriona?'

It was pretty clear that Dad thought, not a lot.

'I just got mad,' I mumbled. 'How could they do that? The dog would have drowned.'

'*You* could have drowned too,' said Dad, 'and then where would you have been?'

I could have said, at the bottom of Millar's pond, but this wasn't the time for jokes.

Tina caught it from Dad too. 'How could you let her do that, Tina?' he asked. 'How could you let her jump into that pond?'

Tina opened her mouth to reply, but Dad immediately patted her shoulder and apologised.

'No, I'm sorry, Tina. I shouldn't have said that. It's not your fault. I know what she's like.'

'Kat just got so mad, Mr McCrumble,' said Tina, close to tears.

'And wet,' I added, trying to wring out my T-shirt.

Dad looked at me, let out a great big sigh and gave me a great big hug.

'Now you're wet too,' I said, my voice a little bit shaky. I hate it when Dad's angry with me. He hardly ever is, so it's much worse when it happens.

'Right.' Dad was brisk. 'Hot bath, Kat, right now. I'll ask Dr Walls to come over as soon as she can. Who knows what you may have caught from that water.'

'The dog . . .'

'Tina and I will look after him. There's nothing broken as far as I can see. Some food and rest and he'll be fine. Now, upstairs. Go!'

I didn't argue. A hot bath sounded like a good idea. I was starting to pong a bit. Stagnant pond water's not the best perfume in the world, and algae in the hair's not a good look either, as I discovered glancing in the hall mirror on my way upstairs.

I collected a big fleecy towel from the linen cupboard and ran a hot bath. I was just about to peel off my wet clothes when Kirsty knocked on the bathroom door.

'I just got back from my shopping and heard the story,' she said when I let her in. 'You're a reckless idiot, Kat McCrumble. When will you ever learn? I've just had to pour your poor father a wee dram to settle his nerves. He knows only too well you could have drowned.' Then she gave me a hug and handed me the bottle of really posh shampoo Dad had bought her at Christmas, and poured great dollops of the matching bubble bath into my bath water. 'Now, get into that bath and don't come out until you're squeaky clean and fit to be seen,' she said.

'What about the—?'

'The dog's fine. There's a grand old fuss being made of him in the kitchen right now. Tina has him on her lap. Poor creature's never had so much attention in his life, I shouldn't think. Imagine trying to drown him. There are some evil people in the world, right enough. But what were you doing near Millar's pond anyway? I thought you'd be keeping off the estate and well out of Ron Jackson's way after what happened with Wilf.'

'Morag said Abandon Hope had arrived at the big hotel and Tina and I were going to sneak up to see if we could catch a glimpse of them.' Funny, I'd forgotten all about them till now. I guess some things are more important.

Kirsty left and I got into the bath and lay and soaked for a little while, but after I'd had a good scrub, I felt OK, and was anxious to get back downstairs to see the dog. Tina was still stroking him, and making soothing noises.

'Hi, Kat,' she whispered as I approached. 'Are you all right?'

'Fine,' I said, and fondled the dog's ears. I could see that, apart from being a bit nervous, he seemed not too bad.

'Sit down, Kat,' said Kirsty. 'Dr Walls has arrived and your dad's in the lounge with her telling her of your escapade.'

'But I'm perfectly all right,' I protested.

'We'll let Dr Walls be the judge of that,' said Dad, appearing at the kitchen door with her.

Dr Walls grinned when she saw me. 'I don't think I've ever seen you so clean, Kat.'

I grinned back. I liked her. She was in the ladies'

'Tug of War' team at the Highland Games and played football in her spare time.

'I hear you've been swimming,' she said, running a professional eye over me.

'Uh huh.' I imagined Dad had told her all the details and I didn't want to go over them in case it set him off again.

Dr Walls sounded my chest and checked my pulse.

'Disgustingly healthy,' she announced. 'You don't seem to have suffered any ill effects so far. But you may have swallowed some pond water, so let me know if you have any stomach pains or if a rash appears.' And she closed her doctor's bag.

'Is that it?' frowned Dad. 'Doesn't she need an antibiotic or something?'

'Not at the moment,' said Dr Walls, 'but there is something I would advise. It's very good for any kind of traumatic event like this.'

'What?' asked Dad.

'A cup of tea and one of Kirsty's scones.'

I grinned. Kirsty grinned. Tina grinned. Dad smiled reluctantly.

'Will you join us, Dr Walls?' said Kirsty.

'I thought you'd never ask,' she said, and, after stroking the greyhound now almost asleep by the stove, settled herself down on a kitchen chair.

I knew I liked her.

Chapter 22

Dad had called Constable Ross as well as Dr Walls, and he arrived just as the tea was being poured. He had a habit of doing that. He said it was his police training. He said tea drinking was the very first thing they teach you at police college. I almost believed him.

But his police training was very obvious when he took Tina and me back through our story of the attempted drowning of the greyhound. He wanted to know every detail: the time and place of the incident, what the men looked like, what they wore, what they'd said, how their voices sounded, and in which direction they'd gone off.

'But they're bound to be miles away by now,' I

wailed. 'I shouldn't have had that bath. I should have gone to the police station and reported the crime right away. It's probably too late to set up a road block now, but you might be able to lift fingerprints from the black sack the dog was wrapped in. Tina brought it back. It's probably in the rubbish bin. And there will definitely be footprints at the scene because the ground round the pond is damp. Tina and I will give you our trainers, so you can examine the soles and eliminate our prints. Also, there may be some forensic evidence: human hair as well as dog hair. Though there won't be a lot of dog hair because greyhounds don't cast that much, and any red hair will most likely be mine.'

Constable Ross looked at me and smiled. 'You have been watching far too many cop shows on the TV, Kat, but, despite that, you have overlooked one vital piece of evidence.'

'What's that?'

'The greyhound.'

I looked over at the dog, now comfortably settled and snoozing in an elderly dog basket Dad had just unearthed. Kirsty had lined it with several of my old jumpers that she'd been trying to persuade me to throw out. I didn't mind; my new friend was welcome to them.

'Do you think he could follow their trail? Help track them down? He's not a sniffer dog, and I really don't think he'd want to see them again. That would be too upsetting for him. Anyway they probably had a car waiting nearby and will be nearly in Inverness by now.'

'Doesn't matter,' said Constable Ross, going over to the greyhound and gently stroking him. The dog stiffened then relaxed. Constable Ross was a friend.

'Come and look, Kat,' he said.

I went and knelt by him while he gently pulled back the dog's ear.

'See here,' he said, and pointed.

'There's a number!' I was amazed. 'A number tattooed on his ear. The poor thing. Did he just have a number; not even a name?'

'I don't know what his name is,' said Constable Ross, making a note of the number, 'but this number will give us the name and address of his owner. Now that *is* a vital piece of evidence.'

'Fantastic,' I said. 'So you'll be able to catch the owner and prosecute him and . . .'

'Throw *him* into Millar's pond. That's what Kat would do, if she had her way,' said Dad.

'Hopefully, we'll catch him,' said Constable Ross, 'but greyhound dumping is a big problem. We don't get so much of it up here in the Highlands. It's much worse in the big towns and cities where there are race tracks. This dog was probably dumped in this out-of-the-way place because his owner has been in trouble before. Some of his pals probably thought they were doing him a favour.'

'Except they reckoned without Kat,' murmured Tina.

Constable Ross nodded. 'Some unscrupulous trainers just dump their dogs when they stop winning races. When they stop winning their owners money.'

'But if they can be traced back through the ear tattoo . . .'

'This dog was lucky,' said Constable Ross quietly. 'He kept his ears.'

'You mean they sometimes cut . . .' I couldn't go on. I felt sick. So did Tina. Her face lost its colour and she wrapped her arms around herself.

Then my temper rose. 'But that's horrendous!' I cried, soothing the dog, who had started at my angry tone. 'How can people BE like that? How could they do that to a gentle animal like this?'

'Fortunately not all people are the same, Kat,' said Constable Ross. 'You *rescued* the dog.'

'I'll never forget you jumping into that pond as long as I live,' shuddered Tina.

'Aye, but you're a tough wee character,' said Dr

Walls. 'I doubt there will be any after effects.'

I looked at Dad's face and saw it grow angry again, as he remembered what I'd done. But I couldn't face another lecture, so I said, 'Look at me, I'm fine. Absolutely fine. I'm a McCrumble. Katriona Mhairi McConnell McCrumble, to give me my full name. But we'll have to give the greyhound a shorter name than that. Any suggestions?'

The ideas came thick and fast. Kirsty suggested Ben. Tina suggested Speedy. Dr Walls thought Algy, after what had been in the water, while Constable Ross favoured Blue. Dad's face cleared and he joined in with a few names of his own, one of which was Lucky.

I relaxed. I'd got out of that one. But I knew Dad had been really angry and I could understand why. Kirsty had told me that just before my mum died he had promised her he would take good care of me. And he has. And I know I really worried him. But I just couldn't let that dog drown without trying to help, could I?

What I want to know is . . . why is it that doing a good deed can get you into so much trouble? Sometimes it's very difficult being Kat McCrumble.

Chapter 23

In the end, I decided to ask the greyhound which name he fancied. I hunkered down beside him again and ran through all the possibilities. He sat, big eyes staring at me, as I tried: Ben, Speedy, Algy, Blue, Lucky. But he didn't seem to fancy any of those. Then I had an idea. He looked so slender, sleek and handsome, that he reminded me of someone. My favourite member of Abandon Hope.

'Micky,' I said. 'What do you think of Micky?'

Tina giggled and the greyhound licked my hand.

'He likes Micky,' I grinned. 'Micky's his name.'

'We need to find out more about greyhounds so we can look after him properly,' said Dad. 'We've never had a rescue greyhound before.'

'I'll do it,' I volunteered. 'Tina has to go home now. She promised to go with her mum up to the Nisbets' farm this afternoon to collect some more wool.'

'But I'd far rather be here,' sighed Tina. 'There's never a dull moment.'

'Not with Kat around,' said Constable Ross, with a smile. 'She keeps me busy. As if I didn't have enough work to do.'

'And speaking of work,' said Dr Walls sadly, eyeing up the remaining scones, 'I'd better get on my way too.'

Kirsty gave all three of them a scone 'carry-out' and they left, grinning.

Meantime Millie, Max and Wilf had been really curious about the new arrival. Millie had sat politely a little way away, her head on one side, just looking at Micky in his basket, but Dad had kept Max and Wilf beside him, in case their antics made the greyhound anxious. Now he took them over to the newcomer.

'Micky might as well get used to them,' he said. 'Micky, this is Wilf. He's a limelight case.'

Wilf stood beside the old dog basket and thumped his tail on the floor. He looked slightly miffed. Here was another animal getting all the attention that was usually his. He thumped his tail again.

'Micky, this is Max,' said Dad. 'He's a headcase.'

Max wagged his tail, pleased at the description, but he couldn't thump his tail like Wilf, so he thought he'd get into the basket beside Micky instead.

'Oh no, you don't, Max,' said Dad, and removed him as Micky began to look fearful again. 'Tell you what, Kat,' he said. 'Why don't you try taking Micky upstairs with you while you find out more about greyhounds. I think he still needs a little more peace and quiet.'

'OK,' I said, and gently coaxed Micky out of his basket. He seemed to trust me and stayed by my side all the way upstairs to my bedroom.

I looked around for something soft for Micky to lie on. He was so thin, I could count all of his ribs. Finally I just pulled the duvet off my bed, made a nest for him and let him lie in that. I know it's unhygenic – Kirsty's always going on at me – but Max sleeps on my duvet most of the time too, and I haven't caught any dreaded diseases yet.

Micky settled himself comfortably on the duvet and watched me with soulful eyes.

'I'm just going to switch on my computer to find out more about you,' I explained. 'You can have another little snooze, if you like. You don't have to worry any more. No one will harm you here. You're safe now.'

Even if Micky didn't understand my words, he seemed to understand my tone of voice, and his eyelids drooped.

While Micky slept I found out that greyhounds are a really old breed of dog, who in ancient times could only be owned by kings. I also discovered they had been worshipped by the Egyptians.

'Worshipped by the Egyptians,' I murmured. 'That'll upset Samantha when she finds out she's not the only superior being around here.'

It appeared too that, because greyhounds are trained to race, they are not allowed to socialise with other dogs.

'But we can make up for that with Millie and Max,' I said.

That ended the pleasant bit of my research. Then I found out that thousands of greyhound puppies are killed before the age of one, if they fail to meet racing standards. I found out that these puppies have been found in trenches after being shot or drowned, and that sometimes the ears . . . I couldn't read any more and sat back in my chair, my stomach churning. Constable Ross had been right.

I stood up, angry tears filling my eyes. Micky

opened his eyes and looked at me. I knelt down on the floor beside him.

'What makes people do things like that?' I asked for a second time.

Micky just laid his head on my lap. He didn't know either.

Chapter 24

News travels fast in Auchtertuie and soon everyone knew about Micky as well as Wilf. The phone never stopped ringing with folks asking how I was and how Micky was. Jinty McCrumble even came round with a tartan dog coat she'd had up in her attic. It would be good for Micky in the wintertime.

Unfortunately the news reached Ron Jackson too. He appeared at the inn next morning. I was just filling some breakfast plates with black pudding and bacon and a couple of fried tattie scones for some Norwegian hitch-hikers who wanted the 'full Scottish breakfast experience', when I heard his voice out in the hall.

'I want a word with you and that daughter of yours,' he said to Dad.

'Then it'll have to wait till after breakfast,' said Dad, who'd just left the kitchen carrying a tray loaded with tea and coffee pots.

But Ron Jackson wouldn't wait and followed Dad into the dining room. I hurried on behind. The dining room was full of guests, thanks to Wilf. Ron Jackson looked round at them and sneered.

'I'm surprised you all want to eat here,' he said. 'Considering the animals that are allowed to roam in and out.'

'The animals are not allowed in here,' said Dad grimly. 'Now, Mr Jackson, if you'd kindly wait in the lounge, I'll see to you in a moment.'

'Oh, Dad,' I muttered under my breath. 'Why are you so polite?'

I would have thumped Ron Jackson but my hands were too full.

'We are here *because* of the animals,' said the Norwegian hitch-hikers. 'We like so much the people who are kind to animals and we like the friendly atmosphere.'

'At least, it was friendly till you arrived, Ron Jackson,' I said, as I laid down the plates.

Dad motioned me to be quiet and ushered Ron Jackson out of the dining room and into the lounge.

I followed. There was no way I was letting Dad cope with this on his own.

Ron Jackson turned on us.

'You have a greyhound,' he said.

'Is he yours?' I asked immediately. I wouldn't put anything past this man. Thank goodness Micky was safely outside with the other animals and being looked after by Donald and Rob.

'No, but I hear he was found by Millar's pond.'

'*In* Millar's pond,' I corrected him, 'where two big brave men had thrown him.'

'You saw them.'

'Yes, I—'

'Then you must have been on the estate. I've warned you about that before, miss. And this time I'm going to make a formal complaint to the police. This time I'm going to prosecute. I'll soon put a stop to you using the estate like it was your own back yard. Your animals are allowed to roam over it and do untold damage, and now you as well. Who knows what tricks you've been up to? I'll have to check the entire estate now to find out. It may have been McCrumble land way back, but now it's owned by C.P. Associates, and the sooner you get that into your thick heads the better.' And he smiled nastily and left.

Wide eyed, I looked at Dad.

'Prosecute?' I said. 'Can he do that? Will I go to

jail?' A sudden vision of our old battered Monopoly board and the GO TO JAIL card came into my mind. 'The men who tried to drown Micky should be the ones to go to jail, not me!'

'Calm down, Kat,' said Dad. 'It's just Ron Jackson sounding off. I'm sure there's no law of trespass even on to a private estate, but I'll check up on it with Willie Ross.'

But I wasn't listening. 'And what about Tina? She was with me. She might get sent to jail too. But it was all my idea, Dad. I'll tell the judge that. Tina didn't really want to go. She's very law-abiding. I talked her into it. I'll take the rap for both of us.'

Dad grinned. 'Take the rap? No more TV for you, Kat McCrumble. Go and clear the plates from the dining room and don't worry about it.'

But I did. Even when the nice Norwegian folks complimented me on their breakfasts, and said what a horrible man Ron Jackson was, I still worried. If I went to jail, who would look after the animals? Who would look after Dad? Who would help with the breakfasts and rescue the toast and the bacon that Dad burnt?

'You're being very silly, Kat McCrumble,' I told myself, giving myself a shake. And I knew that I was, but, even though I kept myself busy with the breakfasts, the worry wouldn't go away.

Chapter 25

I told Donald and Rob and Kirsty all about Ron Jackson.

'He needs a good whack with my broom, that man,' said Kirsty. 'Formal complaint indeed.'

Donald just shook his head sadly, while Rob patted my arm and said, 'Don't worry, Kat. The fellow's a fool, and just a puppet. We know who's really pulling the strings.'

I told Morag too when she arrived with the post. I saw her little red van draw up in the back yard and watched her climb out. Millie and Max immediately bounded up for their treats. But this morning there were two other animals, as Donald and Rob brought over Wilf and Micky. Morag knew all about Micky and had a treat in her pocket for him too. Wilf looked a bit put out till Morag offered him some leaves. Then he and Max had their daily game of football with Max's ball. Millie joined in, but Micky stayed by Donald's side. Donald stroked his head. Micky was still anxious and not yet ready for the rough and tumble of the other dogs. He just didn't seem to know how to play. I felt a lump in my throat and swallowed it quickly as Morag came into the kitchen.

'I might be going to jail,' I announced dramatically.

'Just visiting or staying in?' asked Morag, not bothered in the slightest.

'Staying in,' I said, and for the second time that morning I related the tale of Ron Jackson's visit.

'Och, is that all?' said Morag. 'That idiot's all talk. Likes nothing better than the sound of his own voice complaining about something or other. Anyway, there's no law of trespass in Scotland.'

'I know, but . . .'

'Tell you what, leave it with me. I'll sort out Ron Jackson and his efforts at getting you into trouble.'

And she would say no more.

Dad talked to Donald and Rob about what had happened and decided to phone Constable Ross too. Constable Ross listened, then told Dad he would come in for a chat and a plate of Kirsty's steak pie at lunch-time. Sure enough, at one o'clock on the dot he appeared in the kitchen, sat down at the table and put his hat on a chair.

I eyed him apprehensively.

'You're not going to arrest me?' I asked.

'Why, what have you done?' he mumbled, through a mouthful of the pie Kirsty had placed before him. 'You've not been singing in public again, have you?'

'No. I haven't done anything. Well, nothing much, but Ron Jackson said . . .'

'Never mind about Ron Jackson, Kat,' said Willie Ross. 'He's just a bully. I'm surprised you're not charging him with threatening behaviour, the way he barged in here this morning making false allegations in front of witnesses . . .'

My eyes opened wide and Willie Ross grinned and carried on eating his steak pie.

I sighed with relief; if Willie said it was all right then it was.

'No need for me to bake you a cake with a file in it, then,' laughed Kirsty.

'You could bake the cake anyway,' I said. 'How about a triple-decker chocolate gateau? That's my favourite.'

'I might just do that,' said Kirsty, and began to look out her big baking bowl and her cake tins.

Then she laid out the ingredients and set to work. I love watching Kirsty work. She never weighs or measures anything. Just throws everything together with a couple of handfuls of this, a dollop of that and a wee tate of something else, and it always tastes great. She put the three tins of chocolate mixture into the oven and before long we had a beautiful chocolate gateau, sandwiched with cream and decorated with chocolate buttons. She had to stop me pinching the buttons before they got on to the cake.

And it was just as well because, later on, we had some unexpected visitors for afternoon tea.

I was outside the front door of the inn with the three dogs and Wilf. As usual Wilf was chatting to everyone in sight, enjoying the attention. Max was sitting by him, tongue happily hanging out. We couldn't let Wilf out of our sight now. Someone always had to be near him, just in case. Millie sat quietly at the front door with Micky. I think she sensed his anxiety and had decided to look after him. I was just waiting for Tina to arrive when some daft tourists came along the road. They wore dark glasses, tammies and ginger wigs. They'd obviously been buying Scottish souvenirs. They wandered up to me.

'Are you Kat McCrumble?' they asked.

'Yes,' I nodded.

They looked round, checked no one was looking, then whipped off their wigs and sunglasses.

'We're Abandon Hope,' they said. 'Can we come in and talk to you?'

My legs went wobbly, my stomach did backward flips and my jaw hit the pavement.

The most handsome one stepped forward and held out his hand. 'I'm Micky,' he said.

As if I didn't know!

'H-h-hi . . .' I stuttered. 'I'm Kat . . . but you knew that, er . . . and this is Willie and Milf . . . I mean Millie and Wilf. The dog chewing your trouser leg is Max. Stop that, Max! And this dog is Micky too,' I blushed.

'Called after me, I hear,' the two-legged Micky grinned.

My heart flipped over this time. I could only nod. How did he know?

'We've heard so much about this place, and about you, so we thought we'd come and say hullo. Is that OK?'

OK???

'Oh yes,' I managed to say, when what I really meant was, 'It's fantastic, it's unreal, it's a dream, it's not really happening. Is it?'

Then I remembered my manners.

'Welcome to the Crumbling Arms,' I said. 'Please come in. Would you like some afternoon tea? We have chocolate cake.'

'My favourite,' smiled Micky, and his blue eyes twinkled. My heart danced.

Abandon Hope trooped inside, followed by the animals. They went into the lounge while I ran into the kitchen to tell Kirsty.

'Abandon Hope are here. I can't believe they're actually in the lounge. They would like chocolate cake. Please phone Tina for me and tell her what's happened,' is what I meant to say, but Kirsty says it came out more like . . . 'Abandon chocolate . . . Hope cake . . . lounge phone . . . Tina . . . help!'

But I don't believe her for a minute.

Then I rushed back to the lounge.

By this time Smart was sitting on the floor by the coffee table trying to teach Wilf to play chess, but Wilf was more interested in scattering the chessmen and chewing the chessboard. Max had brought Chris the ball Dad had retrieved from the drain, and they were having a great game of tug-of-war, while Millie was really interested in the flashing lights on Pete's trainers. Two-legged Micky was sitting on the rug in front of the fire stroking four-legged Micky.

'We heard from our waitress, Sarah, about you rescuing the greyhound,' he smiled at me. 'I believe you were out in the estate hoping to bump into us.'

Aha, so Morag had been busy. It wouldn't be easy for the hotel to prosecute me with Abandon Hope on my side.

'Everyone knows everything in Auchtertuie,' I said. 'It's very difficult to keep a secret, even if you wanted to.'

'Well, we just thought your rescue was brilliant,' said Dev. 'We love animals too.'

'And we wanted to shake your hand,' said Pete.

'And perhaps get a photo of you with the animals,' said Smart, 'though I don't think it will be one with Wilf playing chess. Pity.'

'A photograph? You want a photograph of me?'

'Uh huh. Then we could have another photograph with us all together. Would that be OK?'

'Oh yes,' I said, like I had my photograph taken with Abandon Hope every day.

At that moment Kirsty came in with a tray laden with tea and chocolate cake. She was followed by Tina carrying her camera and autograph book.

'This is my best friend, Tina. She was with me when we saw the men trying to drown the greyhound.'

'Hi, Tina,' said the boys.

Tina blushed and grinned. I've never seen her look so thrilled or be so tongue-tied.

'And this is Kirsty. She makes the best chocolate cake in the world.'

'Looks wonderful, Kirsty.'

Kirsty smiled and nodded. I could tell she was pleased.

She put the tray down on the coffee table and Max immediately abandoned his ball and headed for the cake, but Kirsty got there first and headed him off. She cut the cake into neat slices and handed it round.

Max kept his eye on every slice. If a crumb should fall, he'd be ready. He adored chocolate cake.

'I have two rescue greyhounds,' said Micky, through a mouthful of cake. 'They're called Sidney and Slim. They're at home just now with my mum. She runs a greyhound rescue centre. When I was little we lived near a race track, and Mum got so upset about the way the dogs were treated that she decided to do something about it. She rescues the dogs now, and rehomes them with suitable people.'

'That's great,' I grinned. I knew I had been right to choose Micky as my favourite band member.

'Mum also takes the dogs to visit old folks who

don't get out much. Greyhounds are such gentle dogs and the old folks love them.'

And we had more tea and more chocolate cake and chatted, just like we were old friends. The boys talked about their recent tour and about all the places they'd been.

'Though a lot of the time we just see the inside of the concert hall we're performing in,' sighed Pete. 'We could be in London or Glasgow or New York for all we'd know sometimes.'

'Tell us about this place,' said Micky. 'It's really old, isn't it?'

I nodded and told them all about the animals and the wildlife sanctuary, all about Dad and the McCrumble family, all about the Crumbling Arms and its history, and all about C.P. Associates turning out to be a McCrumble. I still could hardly believe that. I also told them about Old Hamish.

'Wow!' said Dev, looking round. 'I'd love to see him. Is he likely to appear at any minute, then?'

'No,' I grinned. 'He usually only comes to warn me if there's trouble ahead.'

'Pity,' said Chris.

Then we took photographs of each other and Tina and I got their autographs. Can you believe that Micky wanted mine as well?

Kirsty brought in more tea and some millionaire

shortbread – these boys could certainly eat – and when that had been scoffed and the crumbs hoovered up by Max, the band stood up to go.

'We need to think about what you've told us, Kat,' said Micky. 'Perhaps we can help in some way. We'll see you at the Auchtertuie Highland Games. We'll be the good-looking ones in the orange wigs.'

Then they donned their disguises again and left.

Tina and I waved them off. We were in a daze. We could hardly believe what had happened. I was still up in the clouds after Tina had gone home and Morag had arrived to help Kirsty with the evening meals.

'We had Abandon Hope here,' I told her, excitedly. 'Can you believe that?'

'Oh yes,' said Morag. 'I was hoping they might come by.'

'Hoping? What do you mean?'

'Well, Henry McCrumble's wife, Lottie's, second cousin, Sarah, had told me the band were very nice laddies who were very keen on animals. They had been asking her all about the local wildlife. So I told her the story about Micky, and she passed it on to them when she served them their food. She's doing lunches at the big hotel this week. The boys obviously did the rest. Sarah was right, they are nice laddies.'

'Micky signed my autograph book with love and kisses.' My voice was dreamy.

'A dog that can write,' grinned Morag. 'Whatever next?' But I was too busy thinking about two-legged Micky to reply.

Chapter 26

The morning of the Auchtertuie Highland Games dawned bright and clear.

'And it'll stay fine all day,' smiled Morag, having her usual cup of tea in the kitchen that morning. Then her blue eye took on its faraway look. 'It's going to be a very busy time here. Lots of noise. Lots of excitement.'

'Och, there's always plenty of excitement at the Highland Games,' said Kirsty. 'I wonder if Willie Ross will win the Highland dancing competition again this year. He's very light on his feet for such a big bobby.'

'Are you going in for the piping competition again, Kirsty?' I asked, though by now I knew quite well that she was. She'd been practising at home and I'd heard that her neighbours had been complaining.

'I certainly am,' said Kirsty. 'I'm much better than last year.'

Well, louder anyway, from what I'd heard.

'What about you, Morag?'

Morag's blue eye had returned to normal and she was back with us.

'I'm in the medical tent in case anyone drops a caber on their toe again, or they trip over their feet in the sword dance. Do you mind that happened one year, Kirsty, when Lachy McCrumble was doing so well till he tripped over the sword, fell off the platform and broke his leg? He hasn't danced since.'

'But you don't "see" that happening again, do you, Morag?' I asked.

'I see a lot of things,' she smiled, and said no more.

'And I *hear* them,' said Kirsty. 'That's the pipe band leading the parade. They'll be along here soon for the pipe major's wee dram. Now, where's the bottle?'

I handed her the flour jar and she took out the malt whisky, poured a generous measure into a crystal glass and put it on to a silver tray.

'Here, Kat,' she said. 'Why don't *you* give it to the pipe major this year.'

'OK,' I beamed. This was quite an honour.

I carried the tray carefully outside. Dad and Rob were already there with Millie and Max and Wilf.

I had no sooner joined them when Tina and her brother, Billy, arrived.

'Very strong drink for very small McCrumble,' said Billy, in his dalek voice. 'That is human being falling-down juice. Be wary. Be wary. Be wary.'

'It's not for me, Billy,' I grinned. 'I'd far rather have Coke.'

Tina looked round. 'Where's Micky?'

'Donald's keeping him in the back yard in case the noise and all the people out here are a bit too much for him.'

'I could look after him,' said Tina, and disappeared into the inn.

I knew she had taken over when, out of the corner of my eye, I saw a man in a white frock nimbly climb up a nearby tree. Donald would get a good view of the procession from up there.

The pipe major, the pipe band and the long line of competitors arrived at the inn.

'Good morning to you, pipe major,' said Dad, as he always does. 'Will you take a wee dram to help you on your way this fine day?'

'I will, sir. Thank you kindly,' said the pipe major, resplendent in full Highland regalia including black busby. It made him look about ten feet tall.

I smiled up at him and stepped forward with the tray. Max decided to get in on the act and ran between my legs. I fell over him. The tray fell with a clatter.

But the pipe major's hand shot out and caught the glass of whisky. He downed it in one. He handed me back the empty glass and winked. 'Long years of practice catching the mace sometimes come in handy, Kat,' he said. And the pipe band and the parade went on its way through the streets of Auchtertuie, heading towards the field where the Games are always held.

We got ready to pile into our old van and Kirsty's mini to get to the field before them. I collected the plastic boxes full of the Mars bar squares I had made to sell in the tea tent. Did I tell you about them? They're my speciality. Easy to make and decidedly yummy. Donald dropped down from his tree. He was going to look after the inn and Micky while we were away. But Tina volunteered to stay and look after Micky too.

'But you love the Highland Games,' I said. 'And Donald will take good care of Micky.'

'I'd rather stay with Micky, just in case,' said Tina.

'Is it OK if I walk him along to my house, once the noise of the parade has gone?'

'Of course,' I said. 'He'd like that, and the exercise would do him good.'

'We can play in the garden,' said Tina. 'Dad has a craft stall at the Games. It'll just be Micky and me and Mum.'

'OK,' I said. 'I'll see you later.' Then a little bubble of understanding floated in my brain. Tina's mum is allergic to cats and also to some dogs, so there are no pets in the house, but greyhounds have a smooth coat and don't cast much, so perhaps Tina wanted to see how her mum would react to Micky . . . I smiled to myself. If it worked out, Micky couldn't go to a better home.

I sat in the back of our old van with Millie and Max and Wilf. I had Max and Wilf on a lead. I was taking no chances. We set off, quite smoothly at first, till we got to the bit of road where it peters out on to the gravel track, then we were bounced around. Dad found a good place to park and I clambered out. Someone was already at the field, waiting for us. Wilf saw her and tugged on the lead, and then bounded towards her. It was Maisie. She held out her arms and had a happy reunion with Wilf. I handed over the lead. Then Rob McCrumble Swift arrived in his hire car and parked beside us.

'Maisie, this is Rob,' I said, and introduced them. Then I left them to get to know each other, and to decide about Wilf's future. It wasn't up to me now.

I headed for the tea tent with my boxes of goodies. Jinty and Kirsty were already there, switching on the big tea urns and setting out the polystyrene cups.

'Och, I hate these awful things,' said Kirsty. 'I like my tea in a proper china cup.'

'Aye, but they save on the washing-up,' said Jinty. 'Hi, Kat,' Jinty smiled when she saw me. 'You're just in time to put out the milk and sugar.'

'OK,' I said, and started filling the jugs and bowls. I had just finished doing that when the sound of the pipe band announced the arrival of the parade.

We all went outside to watch the opening ceremony. Our MSP had arrived. His jacket and kilt were so big it looked like he was wearing someone else's, or perhaps he went to the same clothes shop in Inverness as me. He made a short speech and formally opened the Auchtertuie Highland Games. The fun had begun.

Chapter 27

I wouldn't be needed in the tea tent till later, so I wandered round the field looking at the events starting up. Dad had kept Max on his lead, just in case he decided to trip up the competitors. I could see Max on the other side of the field, excitedly bouncing up and down like his rubber ball. Wilf was hopping along between Maisie and Rob, and drawing a great deal of attention to himself, as always.

Millie came with me. We stopped to watch the shotputters and the caber tossers warming up. They were all great muscly men in white T-shirts and vast kilts, and looked like they'd just stepped out of a porridge oats advert.

The Nisbet boys were watching them too. I think they fancied themselves as caber tossers, but they were so skinny, they couldn't do more than toss a coin. The male Highland dancers were slim too, slim and elegant in their neat kilts and jackets. The jackets all had silver buttons that glinted in the sunshine. I spotted Constable Ross amongst the dancers. He looked different without his police uniform, but, even wearing dancing pumps, his feet were still sizeable. He saw me and came over to have a word.

'Good news, Kat,' he said, fondling Millie's ears. 'I've just heard from my colleagues in Glasgow that they've located Micky's owner and are going to charge him. This isn't the first time he's been caught mistreating animals.'

'Good,' I said. 'I hope they throw him in jail and throw away the key. I hope they boil him in oil. I hope they give him rotten eggs for breakfast. I hope they—'

'He'll probably just get fined, Kat.'

'It's not enough,' I said. 'Not after what was done to Micky and those other dogs I read about.'

'I know.' Constable Ross patted my arm. 'But it's probably all we can hope for at the moment.' Then he went back to watch some of the other competitors dance.

I turned round and almost bumped into the Hobsons, the family who'd been visiting us from London.

'Hullo, Kat,' they said. 'We came back to see the Games, just like we promised. But where's Tina?'

'At home,' I said, and told them all about what had happened to Micky. They were just as upset as I had been. 'But things might work out all right,' I added, and explained how I thought Tina might be able to keep Micky.

'That would be lovely,' said Mrs Hobson. 'I love a happy ending.'

'That's why she always cries at the movies,' grinned her husband. 'A good happy ending needs at least three hankies.'

I left them to enjoy the dancing and went to listen to the piping competition. There were some really good pipers piping songs, marches and laments. The judges were going to find it difficult to choose the best. But they weren't going to find it difficult to choose the worst. When it was Kirsty's turn to play, I saw Henry McCrumble surreptitiously reach into his sporran for his earplugs. And he wasn't the only one. But I clapped as hard as I could when Kirsty had finished. So did everyone else, but probably because they were glad it was over.

'Well, Kat,' Kirsty beamed, when she came over to me. 'What did you think of my playing?'

'Definitely better than last year,' I said. Mind you, last year Max had howled like a constipated coyote when she played, and this year Dad had kept him well away.

Of course Kirsty didn't win.

'Oh well.' She shrugged her shoulders. 'I'll just have to practise even more.'

That would please her neighbours.

Then it was time to help in the tea tent. Kirsty put her pipes into their case and walked back with me. People started to appear looking for cups of tea and home baking, and I was soon buttering scones and pancakes at the speed of light. Morag arrived at one point, looking for a cup of tea for Jinty McCrumble's niece who was in the medical tent.

'Is she all right?' I asked anxiously, remembering the news about the new baby.

'Och, yes,' said Morag. 'She's just putting her feet up and having a wee blether. We were discussing names for the baby. If it's a wee girl she's decided to call her Versace. Either that or Febreze.'

'Versace or Febreze,' I groaned. 'I don't know which is worse.'

Then Maisie came into the tent with Wilf and

Rob. I found them a table near the entrance and looped Wilf's extended lead round a chair, so that Maisie and Rob could keep an eye on him while he played outside.

'Come and join us for a minute, Kat,' they said.

I grabbed myself a Coke and sat down on the chair with the lead.

'I've decided to let Wilf go to Australia, Kat,' said Maisie. 'Now that I've met Rob and talked to him, I think that's what would be best for Wilf.'

I nodded in agreement. 'I hate the thought that Ron Jackson and C.P. Associates will think they've won, but we can't risk Wilf being harmed.'

'Maisie's going to come out and visit him and you must come as well, Kat,' smiled Rob. 'Oz is only a plane ride away and we have some wonderful wildlife too. Have you ever heard of the satin bower-bird?'

I shook my head.

'It's a very shy bird that collects blue things to display in its nest. I lost some lapis lazuli cuff links to that bird once.'

But I could tell by the way he grinned that he hadn't minded at all.

'And,' he lowered his voice, 'I sent in my report about the feasibility of a golf course on the estate.'

'What do you think will happen?' I whispered.

'Nothing,' he grinned. 'Callum McCrumble phoned me right away to say he's not going ahead with the course. Says it would be far too expensive. Anyway, he'd never get planning permission to cut down the old oaks that are there. Donald tells me they're heritage trees.'

I breathed a sigh of relief. 'And Callum still doesn't know you're a McCrumble,' I said.

Rob shook his head. 'He thinks I've been staying at the inn to gain local knowledege.'

I smiled, then it turned to a frown as I saw Ron Jackson enter the tent.

'Well, I hope the tea in here is better than it was last year,' he bellowed. 'Gave me gut rot for a week, it did.'

I stood up to protest, but I didn't get the chance. Wilf heard the bellow and hopped over to see what was happening. He hopped round Ron Jackson, pulling the lead around his legs. Ron Jackson tripped up and the chair fell over on top of him.

'You really should look where you're going,' I grinned, releasing Wilf and holding on to his collar. 'But if you're hurt, you could always go to the medical tent. I'm sure Morag has something there that will sort you out.'

Everybody laughed and clapped as Ron Jackson glowered and left.

'Three cheers for Wilf,' I cried. 'Hip hip hooray. Hip hip hooray. Hip hip hooray.' Everyone joined in and Wilf was delighted. He wasn't sure what he'd done, but he was a star again and that was fine by him.

I'd been keeping my eyes open for some other stars. Abandon Hope had promised they'd see me at the Games, but it was getting late in the day, and the Games were nearly over. Now people were starting to assemble around the main platform for the prize giving. Had Abandon Hope forgotten their promise? Had they been too busy? Had they left Auchtertuie already? I looked up every time someone came into the tea tent, but there was no sign of them. Then Henry McCrumble, the Games organiser, came in.

'Come outside now, everyone,' he said. 'You don't want to miss the prize giving.'

Jinty and Kirsty and I went outside to join Dad and Morag, Maisie, Rob and Millie, and Max and Wilf. I saw Tina on the edge of the crowd with her dad and waved them over beside us.

'How was your mum with Micky?' I asked. 'Did she start to sneeze?'

'Oh, you guessed,' blushed Tina. 'No, Mum's fine. She loves Micky. She's looking after him just now. Do you think I . . . I know it was you who rescued him . . . but would it be possible for me . . .'

'Of course you can have Micky,' I said, and hugged her. She hugged me back, delight written all over her.

Then we watched as Henry McCrumble climbed up on to the platform and raised his hand for silence. 'We've had a wonderful day here at the Games, ladies and gentlemen, and the weather has been good to us. I think Morag ordered it especially.'

Everyone cheered and Morag nodded happily.

'And we must thank all the people who have helped to make today such a success,' he said, and went through a whole list of names.

When everyone had finished clapping, Henry McCrumble cleared his throat. 'Now, there is one more item on the programme for today. A surprise item, but one I think you'll like,' and he walked to the back of the platform and pulled aside the curtain. Five figures stood there wearing dark glasses, tammies and orange wigs.

'Abandon Hope!' Tina and I yelled, and the crowd cheered and clapped as the boys walked forward and took off their disguises. They smiled and took a bow.

Micky stepped up to the microphone. 'Thank you, Mr McCrumble. Thank you, folks. We thought since we were in the area we'd like to play a little song for you today. It's one we've just written and we hope you'll like it. But first of all I'd like to tell you the story behind it.'

And he told everyone about how Tina and I were big fans of the band, and how we'd gone into the estate hoping to meet them, but instead found men throwing a greyhound in a black plastic sack into a vile pond, and about me jumping in to rescue him.

I heard Dad take a sharp intake of breath at that point; he still wasn't happy about it.

Then Micky talked about the plight of the greyhounds and about how proceeds from the song would go to help them. Everyone in the crowd clapped. They liked that. They liked the boys. So did I! Finally Micky went on to say they had written the song specially for me and that the name of the song was 'Simply Kat'.

I could hardly believe it. I stood there in a daze as they sang the song, the music floating over my head somewhere. Dad must have known how I felt because he put his arm round me and gave me a hug. When the song ended everyone clapped and cheered again, but the boys weren't finished.

'We have a couple of prizes of our own to give out today,' Micky said, 'so if Kat and Tina would like to come up to the platform, we'll hand them over.'

Tina and I were shaking as we made our way through the crowd and up on to the platform. Micky kissed us and handed us each a signed album of their latest hits. Then I jumped as flashlights started to pop.

'Smile,' he grinned. 'We organised some photographers. You're going to be all over the newspapers tomorrow.'

'Oh . . . and everyone will read about what's happening to the greyhounds.'

Micky nodded. 'We're in the news just now,' he said, 'so we can use that to draw people's attention to things that concern us. That was the plan we worked out.'

'*I* worked out,' said Smart.

'Show off,' grinned Dev, Pete and Chris.

After that we had lots more photographs taken with the boys. Then I invited them back to the Crumbling Arms for dinner.

'I thought you'd never ask,' grinned Micky. 'Is there any more of that chocolate cake?' The boys insisted that Tina and I go back to the Crumbling Arms with them in their big white limo. We'd never been in one before. It was enormous inside. Big enough to party in. I sat beside Micky. The photographers jumped into their cars and got back to the Crumbling Arms before us. When our limo – I could get used to limos so long as Micky was inside – drew up outside, there was lots of excitement with people cheering and flash bulbs popping.

'Just like I predicted,' smiled Morag, arriving just behind us.

'But you didn't predict Abandon Hope,' I grinned.

'Och, but you have to have some surprises in life, Kat. It wouldn't do to know everything in advance.'

And I suppose that's true. I didn't expect to have a wallaby come to stay with us. I didn't expect to rescue a greyhound. And I certainly didn't expect to meet Abandon Hope and have a song called after me. Nor did I expect to have them sitting round our kitchen table, tucking into one of Kirsty's steak and kidney pies, and eyeing up the chocolate cake on the dresser.

But that's one of the reasons I like living in Auchtertuie; on the surface it looks like such a quiet little place, but underneath there's a lot going on, and you really never know what's going to happen next . . .

Kat's Mars bar squares recipe

Ingredients: 3 mars bars
3 cups of rice crispies
3 oz (75g) margarine
Melted chocolate

- Chop the Mars bars into about six pieces.
- Melt the margarine in a pan and add chopped Mars bars. Heat gently till nicely melted and sticky.
- Remove pan from the heat and add rice crispies. Mix well.
- Empty mixture out on to a greased baking tray and press down with the back of a wooden spoon till smooth.
- When cool, cover in melted chocolate.
- Cut into small squares.

Author's note: Mind your fingers when chopping up the Mars bars, and ask a grown up to help with heating up the mixture. BUT keep an eye on them, and make sure they don't eat too many squares – they're utterly delicious!